Wish You Were Dead

Peter James

Pan Books

First published 2021 by Pan Books
an imprint of Pan Macmillan
The Smithson, 6 Briset Street, London EC1M 5NR
EU representative: Macmillan Publishers Ireland Ltd, 1st Floor,
The Liffey Trust Centre, 117–126 Sheriff Street Upper,
Dublin 1, D01 YC43
Associated companies throughout the world
www.panmacmillan.com

ISBN 978-1-5290-4100-2

7 9 8 6

A CIP catalogue record for this book is available from the British Library.

Typeset by Palimpsest Book Production Ltd, Falkirk, Stirlingshire
Printed and bound by CPI Group (UK) Ltd, Croydon, CR0 4YY

Visit **www.panmacmillan.com** to read more about all our books
and to buy them. You will also find features, author interviews and
news of any author events, and you can sign up for e-newsletters
so that you're always first to hear about our new releases.

For the Brown family – Debbie, Mark and Dani

1

Debbie talked to the dead. 'Hello, boys and girls!' she would greet them all at 10 p.m. every weekday, when she let herself into the silent mortuary, to clean. 'Bet you wish you weren't here!' she would add. They never answered her back – well, at least no one had yet – and she was pretty glad about that.

Her friends asked her how she could stand to work here. Didn't it spook her?

'No,' she would answer. 'The dead don't bother me. It's the living that do. They're much scarier!'

Although, in truth, with the flickering lights and the hum of the fridges, she was always just a little nervous in here. Which was why she liked to chat away, telling them all about her day and asking them about theirs. Most of them, she guessed, had had a pretty shitty day, which was why they were in this place.

She counted from the names on the fridge doors. Eighteen overnight guests. Two more than yesterday. They lay behind the doors on racks of shelves, wrapped in white plastic. Their names were on tags tied to their big toes – except for the occasional ones who arrived with no feet.

Debbie was nosey. As she went about her work, she always wondered what fate had brought each of them here. When she cleaned Mrs Grace's office, she liked to sneak a look at the ledger.

All the details were recorded there. The name, date of death, if known, and suspected cause of death, also if known. Mostly they were known. Heart attack. Stroke. Suicide. Fall from a ladder. Stabbing. Road traffic accident. And mostly they were short-stay, before going off to a funeral home. But a few, names unknown, were here for months. One, badly burnt in a fire, who they had nicknamed Crispy, had been here for two years.

Tonight, she was on a cheeky mission. She had been offered a lovely sum of money – £500 – by Curtis, a dodgy friend of her husband, for some information. Not about one of the guests, but about Mrs Cleo Grace, who ran the Brighton and Hove City Mortuary.

Mrs Grace was going on a family summer holiday later in the year. Could she find out where, Curtis had asked, pressing the cash into her hand.

Debbie loved a challenge, and this one was much easier than she had expected. There, in a stack of papers on Mrs Grace's desk, was a print-out of an email, with pictures, confirming her booking.

Bingo!

Checking to make sure no one was watching, she said, 'No peeping, boys and girls!' Then she took a photo with her phone.

2

If you ask, 'Papa, how much longer?' one more time,
Detective Superintendent Roy Grace thought,
I'll throttle you! He glared in the mirror at his son,
Bruno, right behind him, then at the satnav app.
French names – towns, villages, roads. Every
town, every village, every road. Except for the
one road they wanted. *Rue de Joigns.*

Was there such a road at all, he was starting
to wonder? Could they have been tricked? Might
they be victims of an internet con man? A crook
like one he had recently locked up? Surely not?
Could he and Cleo have booked and paid for a
week's holiday in a French chateau that they
were about to find out did not actually exist?

But of course it did! They'd looked it up on
TripAdvisor, and it had loads of reviews, almost
all positive. It was the rubbish satnav app on his
phone that was at fault here.

Roy had started the journey in their rented car
– a Citroën Space Tourer – in a very happy frame
of mind. He was looking forward to this summer

break in a gorgeous house in northwest France – and to rare quality time with his family. It might be their last family holiday for some while, as Cleo was now five months pregnant.

Yet something was starting to niggle him. It was like a darkness steadily rising inside him, just as the sky, loaded with rain, was steadily darkening outside. It was nearly 4 p.m. and it didn't look as if there was going to be any evening sun today. The tall trees made the road seem even darker, more like night than a summer afternoon.

'Papa, how much longer?' Bruno asked.

Roy caught Cleo's eye and saw she was grinning. She knew how much Bruno was annoying him. Actually, annoying both of them. And she was also pretty sure Bruno kept saying it on purpose – just to really piss them off. It was something the eleven-year-old seemed to like doing. One day, Bruno could put *annoying people* down on his CV as his hobby.

'Not much longer, Bruno,' Roy said. 'It'll be great when we get there, I'm sure.'

And it sure looked amazing in the photos on the internet. *Château-sur-L'Évêque.* A pool, tennis court, bicycles, beautiful grounds, deer park.

Roy took his eyes off the road for a fraction of a second, to glance again at Bruno in the mirror.

But all he could see was the back of his iPad.

In the middle of their rear seat sat their delightful, twenty-eight-year-old Californian nanny, Kaitlynn, who had become something of a family friend. She was sandwiched between Bruno and their two-year-old son, Noah, in his child seat. Roy and Cleo had offered Kaitlynn and her boyfriend, Jack Alexander – a Detective Sergeant on Roy's team – a free holiday. In return she would occasionally look after Noah while he and Cleo went out on some of the long bike rides they'd been looking forward to.

So far as he could tell, Kaitlynn had spent the entire journey either texting or Snapchatting or playing games on her phone. She'd also said that she'd been trying to call Jack to see if he'd arrived safely, but hadn't had any luck getting through to him.

The rain got worse. This was France, mid-August, and a week of solid sunshine was forecast. So far, not a great start. Cleo peered at the map on her phone, also trying to find the road – she'd been trying for ten minutes now. *Rue de Joigns.* Then she shouted out, 'Got it! About three kilometres ahead! The directions the chateau gave us say to turn left off this road, then the entrance will be four kilometres along on the left and we can't miss it.'

'Brilliant!' Roy said. 'Well done, finally! Please God they can give us something to eat, I'm starving.'

'We all are,' Cleo said.

Roy glanced at the clock – 3.45 p.m. 'Try calling them again, just so they know we're only minutes away.'

'Roy, I'm sure if Jack's already there he'll have asked them to keep some food for us,' Kaitlynn said. 'I've texted him as I can't get through on the phone, to tell him that.'

Jack had had to go to Paris yesterday to take a statement from two French police officers for one of Roy's cases that was coming to trial. He was going straight from Paris to the chateau, a 200-kilometre drive, and should have been there by midday.

Roy and Cleo had planned to arrive by 1 p.m., to give them time to enjoy their first afternoon on holiday. But the early-morning Newhaven–Dieppe ferry had been late. Then the satnav had taken them way off track, making them even later. They'd tried calling the chateau several times. Each time all they got was crackle and a faint voice shouting, *'Bonjour . . . bonjour . . .* hello?' Then the phone would go dead.

As Cleo dialled yet again, Bruno announced, reading from his iPad, 'Papa, Mama, listen!'

'Yes, Bruno?' Cleo said.

'It says that next to being in a car, this is where you are most likely to die. Guess where?'

'In an aeroplane?' said Cleo, who did not like flying.

'Wrong!'

'Your kitchen,' Roy Grace said.

'Wrong, that is the third most likely place! It says here the next mostly likely place to die is on holiday. We're in a car *and* we are on holiday. Doesn't that make it probable we are all going to die?'

Roy frowned. Bruno often came up with weird stuff. 'So it's lucky we're not in a camper van, then, Bruno?'

'Why?'

'Because they have kitchens. So we would be in a car, on holiday and in a kitchen!'

They all laughed.

A few moments later, Cleo sounded like she was finally getting through on the phone. 'Hello,' she said. *'Bonjour – pardon – bonsoir!* This is Madame Grace. Hello? Hello?'

Then she took the phone from her ear and turned to Roy, very cross. 'Cut off again. Dead.'

'Maybe the chateau is haunted?' Bruno said. 'Maybe they're all dead too!'

3

'The woods are lovely, dark and deep, but I have promises to keep, and miles to go before I sleep,' Cleo said.

'Where've I heard that before?' Roy Grace asked.

'Robert Frost, the poet.'

'Ah.'

The woods were indeed very dark and extremely deep. Dense forest on either side of them. A creature – barely visible through the torrent of rain – shot across the road in front of the car.

'Was that a fox?' Cleo asked.

'No, a werewolf!' Bruno said.

She looked warily at the forest. 'Kind of spooky enough – I could believe it, Bruno!'

'You'd better!' he said creepily.

Roy began slowing the car. 'We've done over seven kilometres – you said we would see the entrance after four,' he said. 'Didn't they say we couldn't miss it?'

'I didn't see any sign, did you?' Cleo asked, starting to sound tetchy.

'Nope. We must have missed it.'

'How?'

'Dunno, but we must have.' He stopped, turned the Citroën round and accelerated, heading back the way they'd come, the wipers working hard.

'Papa, how much longer?' Bruno asked again.

'Done wee-wee,' Noah announced, suddenly.

'We'll only be a few minutes!' Kaitlynn said, soothing him. 'Just a few minutes then I'll change your nappy.'

'I can do it when we arrive, Kaitlynn,' Cleo said, then halted in mid-sentence and pointed ahead, to the right. 'There! Look, entrance gates!'

Roy slowed the car right down. Two crumbling stone columns topped with round balls. Slightly rusted wrought-iron gates hung wide open, each at a wide angle. A small wooden sign that he had to drive right up close to, in order to read.

CHÂTEAU-SUR-L'ÉVÊQUE

4

'Seriously?' Roy said. 'This can't be it.'

Cleo was looking doubtful. 'Hmmmn,' she said. 'That's the name.'

'So it must be,' Roy replied, equally doubtful, turning in and heading up a steep, tree-lined and potholed carriage drive. 'Let's give this a go and see where we end up. But this can't be a hotel drive.'

'Darling,' Cleo corrected him, 'it's not a hotel, it's a *chambre d'hôte* – French for a posh guest house. Just the owner and his wife, who are our hosts. They probably don't have the money to mend this drive – and they open their house just to make ends meet.'

'Let's hope that the house isn't in the same condition as the driveway!' Kaitlynn quipped.

'I reckon the owners are serial killers!' Bruno said, excitedly. 'We're all going to be murdered.'

'Thanks, Bruno!' Kaitlynn said.

Cleo turned to him with a grin. 'Judging by all the TripAdvisor reviews, there are lots of people who stayed here and didn't get murdered.'

'The owners might have written all the reviews themselves,' he replied.

The avenue wound left, then right, the car bouncing and splashing through deep puddles on what was little more than a cart track. At least the rain had stopped – for now, anyway. They crossed a broken-down bridge over a narrow, swollen stream, and carried on. At last, up ahead were two more pillars, again topped with stone balls.

Beyond, in the murkiness, they could see the silhouette of a huge mansion, with a round tower at one end.

'Is that it?' Roy asked. 'Looks far bigger than in the photos!'

'Wow, it's a palace!' Kaitlynn said, peering up from her phone.

To Roy, the chateau was grand but looked its age, just like the entrance and the bridge they had crossed. It stood on the far side of a circular driveway, with a fancy lake at the front. In the centre of the lake was a fountain, with a statue of a naked cherub – missing its head and an arm – standing on a huge seashell. But the fountain wasn't working.

Their tyres crunched on the gravel, and Roy

pulled up in front of a grand porch, with steps leading up. It would be a lot grander, he thought, with a lick of paint . . .

The front door opened and a mangy grey-and-white mongrel appeared, barking furiously, pulling itself down the steps by its front paws, dragging its hind legs behind it.

'That's terrible,' Cleo said. 'That poor dog.'

'This place isn't quite how it looked on the website,' Kaitlynn murmured. 'Maybe someone touched up the photographs just a teeny, weeny bit!'

Two cats appeared, and sat, like sentries, either side of the door. Their eyes seemed to glow yellow.

'It's horrible,' Cleo said.

'Give it a chance – we're not seeing it in its best light, darling,' Roy said.

'Roy,' Cleo said, 'I don't want to stay here. Let's drive straight out.'

Tired and frazzled after the long and difficult journey, more driving was the last thing he wanted at this moment.

'What about Jack?' Kaitlynn asked, anxiously. 'He should be here. But I can't see a car.'

'He might have parked around the back or in a garage, Kaitlynn,' Roy said. Then, trying to stay positive, he added, 'Maybe it'll look nicer in sunshine.'

'Maybe it'll look even worse,' Cleo replied. 'I vote we leave now.'

'While we can!' Bruno added in a sinister voice.

'Darling,' Roy said to Cleo. 'It's 4 p.m. and we're in the middle of bloody nowhere. And we've paid everything in advance.'

'I'd prefer to be at home rather than here!'

'But Jack's here!' Kaitlynn said. 'We can't just leave him!'

'Of course not, we'll tell him to come with us,' Cleo said.

Before Roy could comment, the front door opened wider and a dumpy, rather stern woman stood there. She looked in her late forties and she was dressed in a drab summer frock and plimsolls. Her face was tight and pinched, behind large glasses, and her mousy brown hair was pulled back into a bun. She reminded him of someone, but at that moment he couldn't think who.

'She looks happy to see us – not,' Cleo said.

'We are a bit late,' Roy replied. 'You know what the French are like about food. They probably had a lovely lunch ready – as we'd asked for – maybe that's why she's looking annoyed,' he said. He was trying hard to be positive, not wanting to start their holiday on the wrong foot.

Although it seemed they were pretty well on the wrong foot already. Both feet, actually.

'Like, it's our fault?' she replied. 'And you're right, Kaitlynn, this place doesn't look anything like the images we saw.'

'Maybe the website pictures were taken a long time ago.' Roy shrugged.

'A *very* long time ago!' Cleo exclaimed.

'I'll go and say sorry in my best French – and explain why we're late. Hopefully they'll be able to rustle something up for us.'

'Otherwise we can eat the dog,' Bruno said. 'It looks like it's on the way out.'

Ignoring him, Roy helped Cleo lift Noah from his child seat, and asked Kaitlynn and Bruno to grab some of their bags. Quietly, to Cleo, Roy said, 'Let's give it tonight, at least. If we don't like it, we can leave first thing in the morning.'

'If we're still alive,' Bruno hissed, overhearing them.

Roy, carrying two suitcases, and Cleo, holding Noah, hurried through the rain and up the steps, into the shelter of the porch, followed by Bruno.

'*Bonjour*, Madame, we are Monsieur and Madame Grace,' Roy said, pretty much using up all he could remember of his schoolboy French. 'We have a booking with you, I think.'

'I am sorry, my English is not so good. You speak French?'

Roy looked at Cleo, then back at the woman. 'My wife – *ma femme* – can speak French.'

Ignoring this, the woman said, a little frostily, 'I am Monique, the Vicomtesse. My husband and I are your hosts. You are very late.' She looked at them all, almost glaring at them. Then in French she added, '*Nous avons préparé la déjeuner comme vous l'avez demandé.*'

Before her job in the mortuary, Cleo had spent a year teaching English as a foreign language to students in Paris. Translating for everyone now, she said, 'The Vicomtesse says she had prepared lunch for us, as we had requested.'

She turned back to the woman and said to her, in French, 'We called you several times, Madame la Vicomtesse.'

The woman replied tartly, also in French.

Cleo translated for Roy, Bruno and Kaitlynn. 'She says no one called.'

Roy frowned at Cleo. *What?*

He noticed the woman's unusually thick eyebrows. They were like two furry caterpillars, and again reminded him of someone, but he could not remember who.

Cleo spoke to the woman in French again, her tone pleasant. Then she quickly translated. 'I just told her we got through several times but kept getting cut off.'

The woman seemed to thaw a little. 'Ah, zis was you? We have problems with the phones today – from the weather.'

'Say we also texted Jack Alexander to tell her,' Roy said.

Cleo spoke to her again in French.

The Vicomtesse's eyebrows crossed, as if the two caterpillars were now in a life-or-death fight. 'Jack who?'

'Jack *Alexander*,' she replied.

The woman shook her head. 'He is not arrived.'

Cleo opened her handbag and pulled out the email confirmation of their booking and showed the woman.

She took it and studied it for some moments. '*Oui*, zis is correct. I have booking for three rooms: Monsieur and Madame Grace, Monsieur Bruno Lohmann, Monsieur Alexander and Mademoiselle Kaitlynn Defelice, and a cot for Noah. *Oui* – yes?'

'That's right!' Roy said. 'But Monsieur Alexander is not here?'

Cleo asked the question in French.

The woman shook her head. '*Non.*'

'Not here?' Kaitlynn said, anxiously.

Roy turned to their nanny. 'I'm sure he will be soon.'

Cleo asked the woman, again in French, 'Is it possible to have a little snack?'

As the woman replied, Roy saw a strange look on Cleo's face a couple of times. When she had finished, again Cleo translated. 'Madame says her husband is a sick man, and they cannot wait for guests who arrive so late. She also says she has set the cot up, as we requested, in the nanny's room.'

'I thought it was going to be in our room,' Roy said, noticing the look on Kaitlynn's face. Her romantic week with Jack had just been ruined.

'Actually, we wanted the cot in our room,' Cleo said in French to Madame.

'I'm fine with him being with me – us – Jack and I – for tonight,' Kaitlynn said.

'Jack must have been stuck in bad traffic,' Cleo said to Roy. 'I'm sure he'll be here soon.'

'God, I hope so,' Kaitlynn said. 'I'm getting really worried.'

'Darling,' Roy said to Cleo, 'can you explain to her the ferry was delayed, then we got very lost. If we're too late for anything to eat, could she tell us if there's somewhere close where we can get something? Explain that we're all very hungry.'

Cleo spoke to her again.

Madame replied with a reluctant nod, her voice sounding a tad more positive.

'She says she will sort out a platter of cold meats and cheeses,' Cleo said.

'*Merci* – thank you, Madame,' Roy said.

'*Merci*, Madame,' Cleo added.

'Could someone give us a hand with our bags?' Roy asked.

The woman looked at him, blankly.

He tapped a suitcase. '*Assistance?*' Then he said to Cleo, 'Darling, can you ask her if someone could give us a hand with our stuff?'

Cleo turned and spoke to the woman. The woman shook her head as she replied.

Cleo frowned for a moment, as if something wasn't right. Then she translated, 'Madame la Vicomtesse says that sadly her husband is in a wheelchair and there is no one else.'

'I do not carry bags,' the woman added, in broken English. 'You must to understand, zis is not hotel.'

You can say that again, Roy thought, smiling inwardly.

'*A* hotel,' Bruno corrected, but the woman didn't hear him.

5

Madame held the door open for them and spoke again in French, looking a tiny bit more friendly as she did so. When she had finished, Cleo translated.

'Madame says the Vicomte – Viscount – and herself would like to welcome us to their home. They hope we will have a pleasant stay. She suggests – as we are hungry and the weather is bad – that she gives us a tour either later or in the morning.'

'Yes, good idea,' Roy said and nodded at the woman with a smile. She didn't smile back.

They entered a huge, poorly lit, oak-panelled hallway, which was lined on both sides by rows of suits of armour. Some were holding shields, some lances. All had their visors down.

'God, they look menacing!' Cleo whispered to Roy.

'They look a lot more friendly than her!' he whispered back.

Bruno looked around excitedly. 'Cool!' he said.

Madame pointed to a grand, ornate staircase, with animal heads on wooden plinths mounted on the wall, all the way up. On the landing at the top stood a whole stuffed stag, the size of a horse, with huge antlers. It was holding its head up proudly.

'I hate people who shoot beautiful creatures like that,' Cleo murmured to Roy.

Roy nodded. 'Me too,' he said. 'It's one thing if they're going to eat them. But to just have it stuffed as a trophy. How brave is that to shoot a defenceless animal?'

'*La chambre* – room – for the boy – is the first and for your nanny and the baby is second.' Then she spoke in French again. Cleo translated when she had finished.

'Madame says that we have been given the honeymoon suite and it has a wonderful view. She's going to sort some snacks out for us now,' Cleo said, but with a slight frown.

'Madame – Monique – can you let me have the Wi-Fi code?' Roy called after the woman.

She turned and gave him a strange look. 'The Wi-Fi is not working. You are on *vacances* – holiday – why you need Wi-Fi?'

She had a point, Roy agreed, privately. But all the same, he didn't like being out of touch with his team.

Leaving Cleo with Noah, he hurried back out to the car, through the rain which had started falling again, to fetch the rest of the luggage they would need for tonight. Then, followed by Bruno with his rucksack, and Kaitlynn holding her bag, they went up the grand staircase, past the stuffed stag at the top, and turned left onto the landing.

'Is that stag real?' Bruno asked.

'It was,' Cleo said.

'Cool!'

The entire landing wall was lined with more animal heads, mostly stags and boars, all on plinths and mounted high up. They struggled along it, as they had been told, until they reached the first room on the right, which was for Bruno.

The boy opened the door and peered into the gloom. Roy, behind him, reached across and found the light switch.

One of the bulbs in the round, wooden chandelier blinked on and off with a crackling sound, then stayed on. Despite the size of this mansion, the room was tiny, a single brass bed almost filling it. It was covered in a worn, candlewick spread. Just beyond the foot of the bed was a plastic shower curtain.

'Urrr!' Bruno exclaimed, looking up at a spider hanging from the lampshade.

Roy and Cleo exchanged a glance.

'Surely they have a bigger room than this?' she said, grimly.

Roy stepped forward and pulled aside the shower curtain, to reveal a quaint toilet, shower stall and a washbasin. He'd seen bigger prison cells than this room.

'Where's the television?' asked Bruno. 'And what is the Wi-Fi code?'

'First thing tomorrow,' Cleo said, 'we're out of here.'

Kaitlynn and Jack's room was bigger, with the cot they had requested. Leaving the nanny to sort Noah out, and not letting Cleo carry anything heavy, Roy lugged their bags along the corridor. He reached the bottom of a very narrow, very steep spiral stone staircase. It was almost dangerously steep, he thought.

He left one bag at the bottom, planning to return and get it. They began climbing, winding around anti-clockwise. Roy carried a heavy bag with his right hand, gripping the metal handrail with his free left hand. He told Cleo to hold tightly on to the rail, too. There was a real danger of them falling backwards if they let go, he realized. It was that steep.

They climbed on, going round and round. Halfway up, they stopped on a small landing, putting down their bags to have a rest. 'The view had better be bloody worth it!' Roy said, panting heavily.

'This place is a deathtrap,' Cleo wheezed. 'I've not seen a single fire extinguisher anywhere and—'

She stopped, mid-sentence. Inches above her head was a large, old fuse box, with a handle on one side. An electrical cable, a good inch thick and wrapped in ancient-looking rubber, ran from the bottom of it and into a hole drilled at the back of the staircase.

More cables trailed from the box, thick, heavy-duty flex with the ends exposed, showing old copper strands. It was as if there had once been some major rewiring of the house planned, but then abandoned.

'This looks like the main fuse box for the house,' Roy said. 'At least we know where to come if one blows,' he said, trying to sound positive.

'And if a fuse blows, I'll tell you where you can find me,' Cleo said. 'Back in the car, with all bags packed.'

He grinned.

'It's not funny, Roy.'

'Don't worry, we had a fuse box just like that when I was a child. If a fuse blows, I'll be able to fix it.'

'Really? Without frying yourself and burning the house down?'

'Trust me.'

Roy's father, also a police officer, had been a DIY expert, rewiring their family home himself – with Roy, then a small boy, helping. He remembered some of what he had done with his dad. It had always been useful. Over the years he'd saved a lot of money on workmen by being able to fix stuff in the house, particularly anything involving the electrics.

Staring at the fuse box, Roy thought there was no way this could have passed any recent safety test. It was truly ancient – thirty or forty years old at least. And their room was above this! It was going to be like sleeping above a bomb. To make it worse, he'd also seen no fire extinguishers anywhere in the house.

Was there a lightning conductor? He doubted it. God forbid the tower got struck in the lightning storm they'd seen in the distance on their way here. But then again, he tried to comfort himself, it had stood here for at least four centuries – and it sure felt robust.

They carried on up, clinging to the handrail, lugging their bags. Seventy-two steps, Roy had counted, by the time they reached the top, very out of breath despite his good fitness level. Cleo was breathing heavily, too. 'Glad I'm not drinking,' she gasped. 'Wouldn't fancy that climb after a few glasses of wine!'

A thick oak door faced them, with a huge brass key sticking out of its ancient lock. He turned the handle, pushed, then pulled, but the door wouldn't budge.

'Try unlocking it, darling,' Cleo said, teasing.

He twisted the key and it stuck, before finally turning with a click as loud as a gunshot. He tried the handle again and pushed hard. The door opened stiffly inwards, making a loud scraping sound. 'Nothing like making us feel welcome!' he said.

Cleo shook her head. 'I can't believe this place. Haven't they heard of maintenance?'

Roy put his arms around her waist and nuzzled her neck. 'At least we've been given the honeymoon suite. We'd better make good use of it!'

'I'm not sure about Madame,' she said.

'She's not exactly the most charming of hosts.'

'No, it's not that. It's her French.'

'What do you mean?'

'She gets some words wrong. The first thing she said to us was that she'd prepared lunch for us. *La déjeuner*, she called it. It should be *le déjeuner.*'

'Are you sure?' Roy said.

'Yes.' Cleo frowned. 'The thing is, no French person would ever get that wrong – they just wouldn't. And she's got several other words wrong.'

'Maybe she isn't French, darling – perhaps she's from somewhere else in Europe and it's her second language.'

'Perhaps. I'll ask her later.'

They entered a huge oak-panelled room that was as dimly lit as the hall, even after Roy had turned on all the lights, including the bedside lamps. There were tall windows with chintz drapes and a very high four-poster bed. The polished wooden floorboards were covered with faded Oriental rugs. On the wall facing the bed, beside the door to the en suite bathroom, was a life-size crucifix, with a Christ who was truly in pain. But the view out across the grounds, even in this weather, did have the wow factor.

Cleo had a quick peep into the bathroom. 'Roy, we *must* take some photos, this is mad. The bath has to be a hundred years old.'

He followed her in and looked at the enormous tub mounted on feet like lion paws. 'Room for two!' he said. 'We could have a bath together later, with a glass of champagne.'

She patted her swollen belly. 'I wish.'

Then, peering in at the cracked enamel, with deep-brown stains down the sides, Roy said, 'On second thoughts, perhaps not.'

Back in the room, climbing up onto the bed, he said, 'If this is the honeymoon suite, I reckon any newlyweds who wanted to consummate their marriage in this room would need to be mountain-climbers.'

Cleo, smiling, looked at him. 'I just can't believe this place. It is so not what I was expecting. I'm sorry, I've really screwed up.'

'Maybe it will all look different tomorrow, in sunshine, my darling.' He jumped down and went over to one of the windows.

'Yes, my love. In our rear-view mirror. We are so not staying – this whole place is giving me the creeps.'

'Let's at least give it a chance,' he said.

'Really? Why?'

'Apart from anything else, because we've paid – and I doubt Madame Charming is going to give us our money back.' He smiled. 'Hey, come and have a look out here!'

She joined him at the narrow window. They stared down at acres of lawn, with forest at the edge. 'Quite a view, isn't it!' he said, trying to get her to perk up.

'The view's fine,' she said. 'It's all the rest of it that's a bit shit.'

'Darling, come on. The reviews on the internet were good – four-star average – and loads of them. Let's see how it looks tomorrow when the sun's out?'

'Hmmmn.'

'Let's unpack later – our lovely Madame said she was sorting out something to eat.'

'You go ahead, darling. I've got to freshen up – and check on Bruno and Kaitlynn and Noah. Make sure there's something for Jack, too; he must be here soon.'

Roy glanced at his watch. 'This is not like Jack – I hope to hell nothing's happened to him. I've tried sending him another text, but it won't go.' Then, mimicking Madame's accent, he said, '*The Wi-Fi is not working. Why you need Wi-Fi, you are on holiday?*'

Cleo shrugged. 'She has a point.'

'She does, gorgeous.' Roy grinned, wickedly. 'Her nose – it's very pointed!' He pinched the end of his own nose and stretched it. Imitating the woman's accent again, he said, 'I am ze wicked witch of zis house!'

As Cleo laughed, Roy left the room and hurried downstairs. Choral music, playing at an almost deafening volume, greeted him as he reached

29

the hall. It seemed to be pounding at him from the ceiling and the walls, making him feel as if he was in a cathedral.

Through a doorway he could see Madame, oddly changed into a waitress's black-and-white tunic. She was holding a tray on which sat two slim glasses filled to the brim with champagne. He went through. Behind her was a spread of cheeses, cold meats and fruit, laid out on vast silver trays on a grand dining table.

He accepted the glass gratefully, deciding that things were, perhaps, looking up. '*Merci!*' He raised the glass and said, 'Cheers!' Then, remembering more words from his schooldays, said cheers again, this time in French. '*À votre santé!*'

Her lips smiled but not the rest of her face. 'Dinner tonight will be at a quarter to eight. Your family will please be on time.'

'Of course. May I see a menu – and a wine list?' he asked. And instantly saw the stony look on her face.

Her smile frosted over. 'Menu? I'm afraid we do not offer a choice. Tonight we have foie gras, followed by fillet steak, with cheese and dessert after.' Her accent was so thick that he almost had to translate her English.

'Ah,' Roy said slowly. 'We have a bit of a

problem – you see, neither Kaitlynn nor my wife eat meat – they are fine with fish.'

The woman frowned for a moment, then said, stiffly, 'Maybe we can give them *escargots*?'

'Snails?' Roy translated. 'I don't think so.'

She suggested another dish, in French, which he also recognized. 'Frogs' legs?' he said with a shudder. 'No, thank you! They would be very happy with just vegetables,' he said, trying to keep things pleasant.

'They eat potatoes?'

He nodded. 'Yes, they like potatoes. And perhaps a salad?' He nodded at the platter of cheeses. 'Like that would be fine for the rest of us.'

'Huh.' She turned away and walked towards a door. Then she stopped, turned back and said, with a strange smile, 'You English, you *Rosbifs*, you are all the same with your strange eating.'

She left without another word.

6

In the pitch darkness, Jack Alexander was trying to think clearly, and his blinding headache made that hard. His skull felt like it had an ice pick sticking into it. His shoulders ached like hell. His wrists were bound tightly together in front of him by what felt like cable ties, which cut painfully into him. The ties were attached to a chain linked to a heavy metal ring fixed to the wall.

Try as he could, he was unable to get any slack to free the bindings. They felt like they were cutting into his wrists deeper and deeper. Was this what it would have felt like to be locked in a medieval torture chamber, he wondered?

He could only breathe through his nose, because his mouth was taped shut, preventing him from crying out. He was painfully hungry and very thirsty. And he needed to pee. He fought that, but it was getting harder with each passing minute. He had no idea how long he had been down here – wherever *here* was. Hours, for sure, since he had driven up to the front entrance of this horrible dump of a chateau.

Some holiday this was turning out to be, he thought, grimly.

All he could remember was walking up the steps to the front door. It had opened and he had seen an angry woman with her arm raised, holding what looked like a cosh, a split second before she brought it crashing down.

Then darkness and silence.

Until a short while ago, when he had heard voices. Familiar voices. Roy Grace. Cleo and – he was sure – Kaitlynn. Up until then the only sounds had been the occasional pained bark of a dog.

Worried out of his mind for them all – and especially for Kaitlynn – he had tried to shout out to them, to warn them to get the hell away, but no sound would come out of his mouth.

There was another surge of acute pain in his bladder. He clenched tight, fighting it with all his strength, willing it to pass. Thinking. All the time thinking. This must be a nightmare. The worst dream ever. He would wake up soon. Please.

Please.

Now he could hear music. Like a church choir singing.

Somehow, somehow, he had to warn them all to get away. To get help.

He also had the feeling that, wherever he was, he was not alone. He could sense other people in here with him. They were in a cellar, he guessed, from the cold and damp. He wanted to call out to them but, unable to move his mouth, he could only make the faintest of grunting sounds.

7

'Don't eat too much, everyone,' Roy Grace warned. 'Dinner is in just a couple of hours' time!'

Bruno, ignoring him, was wolfing down slices of bread heaped with salami and cheese, and slurping a large glass of Coke. Cleo, who had Noah on her lap, was hungrily tucking into the salad and bread. Roy was trying to hold back, but the cheeses and fruit were so good and the bread so fresh, and the red wine was very drinkable.

Once Jack joined them, maybe this place would be all right after all, he thought.

Kaitlynn had picked at the fruit but eaten little. She sat at the table with her phone, dialling and redialling, shaking her head each time. 'I asked Madame if I could use her landline, but she said – I think – a lightning storm knocked their phone and internet out. Can you believe it, no Wi-Fi or mobile signal?'

'Which might be why we had such problems

getting through to them from the car,' Cleo suggested.

'This room is so creepy. And how am I supposed to join in any games?' Bruno mumbled through a mouthful of food. 'No internet is just shit.'

Roy was about to tick him off for his language but caught Cleo's warning eye and stopped. Bruno was right, it was damned creepy. This huge, gloomy, windowless room in the centre of the house was panelled in dark wood, with a high, vaulted ceiling. It felt like they were in a chapel.

There were silver candlesticks on the table, with unlit church-like candles. At the far end was an alcove in which stood a life-size marble statue of a naked man on a plinth, looking down on them. He had one arm raised and folds of what looked like fabric draped over the other arm. Was he a Greek god, Roy wondered? He'd never been good on mythology.

'Something must have happened to Jack,' Kaitlynn said, sounding really worried and upset. 'This is so not like him.'

'Perhaps he's been abducted by aliens?' Bruno suggested. 'You know, French ones?'

'That's really not very helpful, Bruno,' Cleo said.

'They happen,' he said, defiantly. 'Alien

abductions. I read it in a magazine. People driving along one moment, and the next, whoosh – they're gone, sucked up into a space-ship! The next time anyone sees them they're all totally weird.'

'Yeah, and I read about small boys being eaten by a tribe of monsters in the woods,' Kaitlynn retorted. 'How come they missed you?'

'Hey!' Roy said. 'Cool it. Bruno, we're all concerned about Jack, OK? It's not funny.'

'Really?' Bruno answered. 'Is that why we're all sitting here stuffing our faces, if we're all so concerned?'

Roy stood up, holding his phone. 'I'll see if I can get a signal outside.'

'Darling, finish your food first,' Cleo said. 'You've not eaten anything for hours.'

'I'm just going to the front door to see if I can get a better signal. I'll be right back.'

He walked out into the hall. Stepping into the porch, he saw in front of him a wall of pelting rain, and then a streak of lightning. Checking his phone, there was still no signal. All the same, he tried calling Jack. But nothing happened. He tapped out a text and tried sending it.

It would not go.

He went back into the hall, looking warily at all the suits of armour. He felt like each of them had someone inside, watching him through the eye slits, as he walked back towards the dining room. But just before he reached the entrance, he saw a door off to the right and, curious, went over to it.

It led into a huge drawing room, furnished with antique sofas, tables and display cabinets full of silverware and ornaments. Three of the walls were hung with oil paintings in gilded frames. Some looked like portraits of ancestors, others were landscapes, hunting scenes and beautifully painted pictures of horses and dogs.

On the fourth wall, above an ornate marble fireplace, were dozens and dozens of framed photographs, all signed. Among them were a number of celebrities he recognized – rock stars and actors, some living, some long dead – and some faces he did not recognize. It looked like a Hall of Fame of past guests.

Each photo had a brief, scrawled message. One picture was of the late, great actor Humphrey Bogart, with his trademark cigarette in his mouth. He was standing in the hallway of this chateau, his arm around a suit of armour. *'Great stay in this amazing place! Got a new buddy!'* Next to him was a black-and-white photograph of the late Vivien Leigh. *'Such a great time here. Such history!'* A short distance away was a photo of

Peter Sellers. *'Much preferred it here to Balham!'*

As Roy continued admiring the photographs, he noticed a face he recognized but could not immediately place. It was a man in his fifties, with close-cropped hair, standing with his arm around a wild-looking woman. *'What a gem we've discovered!'*

Roy looked at the signature but couldn't read who it was. He looked at the face again, puzzled. He had an almost photographic memory, particularly for faces, which had always helped him in his career with the police. But, however hard he tried, he could not think who the man was.

Maybe he was tired from the long drive, or it was the booze – probably both, he decided. He went back into the dining room and sat back down next to Cleo. 'Wow!' he said. 'I just took a look in the amazing drawing room. You have to go in there – there are photographs of dozens of major celebrities who've stayed here!'

'Well, I hope they got a better greeting than we did!' she retorted.

8

Half an hour later, Roy and Cleo went back to their room. Both were out of breath from the climb up the tower's seventy-two steps. Roy gasped, 'Happy holiday, my love!'

'Some holiday! So far it feels more like we're in some fly-on-the-wall film about the Holiday From Hell!'

Cleo knelt and unzipped her suitcase. 'Poor Kaitlynn's looking frantic. What are we going to do about Jack?'

'If he's not here by dinner time, I'll nip down to the road in the car and hope to get a phone signal there. Jack's a smart guy, I'm sure he's OK. He's probably stuck in a mighty traffic jam or broken down. Or he might have just got delayed in Paris with all that red tape the French police have. Don't worry, he'll rock up.'

'If he can ever find this sodding place,' she said.

'True!'

'Dinner – yuck – I wish I hadn't stuffed myself

with all that food – I'm full – need to do some exercise. Perhaps we could go for a walk?'

Roy peered out of the window at the falling rain, then gave her a naughty look. 'Perhaps we could do some other form of exercise?'

She tilted her head and grinned back. 'Oh, what did you have in mind exactly?'

He took a step towards her and put his arms around her, nuzzling her neck. 'This sort,' he murmured.

She eased herself away, gently, still smiling. 'I like your thinking, but I vote we unpack first. Just our wash stuff and a change of clothes for tonight. Leave everything else for a quick getaway in the morning?'

'Sounds like a plan. But maybe if Madame puts on a nice meal we'll feel different.'

'Really? What planet are you on? Or did you get abducted by Bruno's aliens and have your brain messed with, darling? This place is not for us, don't you think?'

'Maybe it'll grow on us.'

'Maybe,' she said, digging through her clothes. She pulled out a slinky black dress, then stood up and held it against her body. 'What do you think – this tonight?'

He tilted his head one way, then the other. 'I have a problem with that dress.'

'You do?'

He nodded. 'Yep – the moment you put it on, I'm going to want to rip it straight off and ravish you!'

She punched him, playfully. 'OK, Mr Big Seducer, what about you, then? What do you have to wear tonight that's going to make me want to rip it off without undoing the buttons?'

He grinned again and dug into his bag. 'Let's see what I can find!'

She walked over to him and kissed him. 'Actually, Detective Superintendent, I like you best with nothing on at all.'

'That can be arranged,' he said.

'Good.' She glanced at her watch. 'We have just under an hour.'

Eagerly tugging off his T-shirt, he put his arms around her. 'So it will have to be a quickie!'

She gave him a very mischievous smile.

9

At 7.45 p.m., smartened up for dinner, they went down into the hall – Cleo in her black dress, her bump showing, and Roy in a dark jacket over a white shirt. Both were in a very much better mood. A choral chant was blasting out. It was playing far too loud and seemed to be coming at them from every direction.

Madame stood in the entrance to the dining room, holding a huge silver tray, on which sat three champagne flutes. Roy took a glass, but Cleo asked if she could have some water. 'I can't drink, I'm afraid. I'm pregnant.'

The woman looked at her, puzzled.

Cleo patted her tummy and explained in French.

Madame responded with a thin, 'couldn't care less' smile, followed by '*Bon appétit*', and stepped aside to allow them to enter.

Bruno and Kaitlynn were already there, seated either side of the dining table. The room was even more dimly lit than before. A baby monitor sat in front of Kaitlynn, who was stabbing at the keys on her phone again. Flickering candles burned in silver holders on the walls and on the table, sending shadows jumping around the room. Glass decanters of white and red wine were also on the table.

Madame ushered Roy and Cleo to their places, side by side at the head of the table, facing the statue of the naked man with the marble drapes over his arm. There was another figure a short distance in front of the statue. Low down and motionless was a man in a wheelchair, wearing dark glasses. He was heavily bearded, with a mane of silver hair that covered his forehead and tumbled down to the shoulders of his velvet jacket. He wore a bright-yellow cravat.

The woman walked across, held out an arm towards him and spoke to them all in French. When she had finished, Cleo translated.

'Madame says she would like to introduce her husband, the Vicomte Michel du Carne de Chabrolais, fifteenth Vicomte Joigny. She says he speaks even less English than she does. She is sorry that he is not able to get up from his wheelchair. He's recovering from a stroke. But Madame says he is proud to be our host for our stay in his beautiful Château-sur-L'Évêque, and if there is anything we need, to please ask either of them.'

Roy filled Cleo's glass with sparkling water, then raised his flute of champagne at the man in the wheelchair. Cleo and Kaitlynn raised their glasses, too.

'Cheers!' Roy Grace said.

The Vicomte, clearly struggling, managed to raise an arm a little in response.

Roy turned to the nanny. 'Still no luck with Jack?'

She shook her head, looking very upset. 'I've been outside and tried there, too. There's just no goddamn signal.'

'OK,' Roy said. 'Look, Kaitlynn, I'm sure there's nothing to worry about. Jack's a big boy and he knows how to look after himself – he'll have a perfectly good reason for this. But before I have anything more to drink, I'm going to drive back down to the road and see if I can get a signal there. If Madame serves the starter, don't worry about me, I'll have it when I get back.'

But before he could get up, Madame appeared as if from thin air with her most pleasant smile so far. She was carrying another huge silver tray, on which was laid out a generous platter of smoked fish. 'For Madame and Mademoiselle,' she said, smiling at the two women.

Their hostess left through a door and returned with another equally large silver tray containing the rich goose-liver pâté, called foie gras, sweet pickles and rich brioche buns. 'For Monsieur Grace and Monsieur Bruno!' she said, laying it down.

Roy had recently read about how foie gras was created and had vowed never to eat it again. He was only doing so now to try to be close to his son, who was already tucking in.

Madame topped up their glasses, then stepped back, folded her arms and stood a short distance from them, like a sentry. 'Please you will enjoy,' she said. *'Bon appétit.'*

'Merci!' Roy said, followed by Cleo who politely said the same.

Roy ate a mouthful of the rich pâté. Then he checked his phone again. Still no signal. He looked at Kaitlynn. She shook her head, then glanced at her own phone. 'I still don't have a signal.' She slipped away from the table to go and check on Noah. And, no doubt, Jack.

'Papa, do you know how foie gras is made?' Bruno said. 'It's gross! They force-feed a goose, making its liver swell until—'

'Bruno!' Cleo said firmly. 'We really don't need to know right now, OK?'

Roy stood up. 'Right, what I'm going to do is drive back down towards the road, where we last had a signal, and try Jack from there.'

'Roy, finish eating, at least,' Cleo said.

'Darling, he might be broken down somewhere and going nuts trying to contact us. I'll be back in ten minutes, OK?'

He told Madame the foie gras was delicious and that he would be back to finish it. Then he left the dining room and hurried out through the front door into the porch. And stopped. A wall of rain was pelting down even harder than before. There was another brilliant flash of lightning and it was followed, almost instantly, by a massive crash of thunder. It was as if the sky above him had been torn apart.

The storm was right overhead. He remembered something his dad had taught him many years ago. If you could count five seconds between the flash and the thunder, the storm was one mile away. If the thunder followed the lightning instantly, it meant danger, it was right overhead.

Should he go back in and wait for it to move away? That would be the sensible thing. But poor Kaitlynn was desperate, and in truth he was now very concerned about Jack, too. He glanced warily at the sky, then ducking his head, he sprinted across to their Citroën. He gave the driver's door a hard yank.

It was locked.

Shit. Bugger. He remembered he'd left the keys

all the way up in his room. Great! Seventy-two very steep steps both ways and no sodding lift.

There was another brilliant flash and a crash that rippled on and on, as if the sky was now being ripped into a thousand pieces. Holding his breath, he ran back to the porch, stepping inside gratefully, and totally drenched. Then he raced back up the staircase, passing the stag that stood at the top like a sentry, and along the landing to the spiral staircase. Hauling himself up every step with the handrail, he reached the top of the tower. Drenched in sweat as well as rain, he stopped to get his breath back as he stood outside their room. Thunder again crashed outside. This time it sounded as if a million metal dustbins were banged together at the same moment.

Grabbing the keys from the dressing table, he walked carefully down, again using the handrail. As he stepped back out into the porch, there was another lightning flash. He counted. *One . . . two . . . three . . .* then *boom.*

That meant the storm wasn't right overhead any more.

He dashed back over to the car, pressing the key fob button to unlock the doors on the way. But nothing happened. He tried again. Rain pelted down like he was standing under a shower, drenching him even more. Still nothing. Was the battery in the fob dead?

He pushed the key into the door lock and had to twist hard to turn it. The door unlocked with what seemed an unwilling click. He pulled it open, jumped in and pulled it shut against the weather. He was a little surprised that the interior light had not come on. Then he looked at his phone once more. Still no signal. He tried sending another text to Jack, but just like the previous three, he got an *unable to send* message.

He would have to drive down to the road to get a signal, he thought, and pushed the key into the ignition. But when he turned it there was just a dull click from somewhere in the car's electrics.

He tried again. Another click. Nothing else.

Flat battery. *Shit, shit, shit.* Of all the times to get one . . . This bloody car was almost brand new, with less than three thousand kilometres on the clock. There had to be an electrical fault – a short of some kind. Hadn't the rental company checked it out properly? Or had the heavy rain somehow got into the wiring? If they'd been in England, he could have called out the RAC. Was there an emergency help number somewhere in the car's paperwork, which he'd shoved into the glove locker after they'd left the rental place?

Using his phone torch – and suddenly noticing, to his dismay, that he had less than 20 per cent charge remaining – he found a bunch of stapled papers. Scanning through, he found the emergency number for Europe.

Duh! No signal. He couldn't bloody call it!

All the same, he tried.

With no success.

10

God, how long had he been here now, Jack wondered?

Suddenly, he heard the sound of a door creaking open on rusty hinges. He held his breath. At last, was someone coming to release him?

A bright light swept across the room. He caught a fleeting glimpse of two other figures, on the far side, who also seemed to be tied up, gagged and chained to the wall. He tried to call out, but the sound was trapped by the tape across his mouth.

The light went off. He heard the creak of the hinges again, then the sound of a door slamming.

Think, think, think. His mind was spinning. There had to be *something* he could do.

But what?

Who was this person with the torch? Why were they doing this to him and the two others in here he had seen – a man and a woman? Who were these two people?

He kept on trying to free himself, to yank the chain from the wall, on and on and on, until he was dripping with sweat and too exhausted to continue.

And all the time he was thinking, over and over again. Wondering. Who the hell were his captors? Why were they doing this to him? What did they want?

And an even bigger fear. Kaitlynn. Was it possible these maniacs, whoever they were, were doing the same to her? And to Roy Grace and his family?

He wrenched again, with all his strength, pulling at the ring, and ignoring the worsening pain in his wrists from the ties.

11

Soaked through, his hair stuck to his head, and feeling like a drowned rat, Roy squelched back into the dining room. From a distance, he could see his plate had been cleared away. Madame was no longer there. Her husband sat, silently and without moving, in his wheelchair.

Partly, he was relieved he did not have to eat any more of the foie gras, but at the same time he was starving and annoyed that the brioches had gone.

Cleo turned to him as he stood over her. 'Any luck, did you get through?'

He shook his head. 'We've got a sodding flat battery.'

'What?'

'The car wouldn't start – the electrics are dead.'

'How – I mean, it's almost brand new, and it was fine all the way here, wasn't it?'

'Either the battery wasn't charging, which means the alternator has packed up – which could explain why my phone wasn't charging

– or there's a short. Right now it's kaput!' He shrugged and went over to the man in the wheelchair.

'Monsieur le Vicomte,' he said, 'do you have the number of a garage? We have a problem with our car.'

Their host tilted his head up a fraction. In slurred, broken English, he replied, 'You have problem with your *voiture* – your car?'

'Yes – *oui*. It won't start. The battery is flat. Do you by chance have a charger? Or jump leads?'

The Vicomte gave him a weird shrug, with just one shoulder, as if the other wouldn't move. 'There is no garage who will come at this hour. Tomorrow – in ze morning – I call for you, if the phone works. Tonight, you do not need your car, surely, Monsieur? Relax and enjoy the wines from our ancient cellar!'

'I need to drive to get a phone signal – to call my nanny's boyfriend, who should be with us. Jack Alexander. We do not understand why he is not here.'

'Jacques Alexander?'

'Yes – *oui*.'

The old man shook his head. 'Tonight *non*, *rien*, nothing. I am sorry. Tomorrow we try, yes?'

Roy was surprised that he spoke better English than Madame had said. 'Thank you – *merci*.'

Madame appeared through a doorway, holding a huge silver tray loaded with plates of food. There was a wonderful smell.

Roy went over to the table and told Cleo what had been said.

'There's nothing else we can do, darling,' she said. 'We'll have to wait until the morning. Go up and change – you'll catch your death of cold.'

Nodding reluctantly, he hurried back up the landing, the delicious smell of food following him, and yet again hauled himself up the tower's spiral staircase. He could have sworn it was even steeper and that there were more steps than before.

In their room he towelled his hair, dug out a fresh pair of jeans, a shirt and dry trainers from his bag. When he returned to the dining room a few minutes later, Cleo and Kaitlynn had salmon steaks, French fries and bowls of salad in front of them.

Moments later Madame came back in with the same tray loaded with plates of fillet steak and fries for himself and Bruno.

The steaks were perfectly cooked and delicious – and the chips were amazing. They were followed by more of the wonderful cheeses they'd had earlier, that Madame said were all local. Then a dessert to die for – meringues swimming in a pool of warm, thin, creamy custard. *'Îles flottantes!'* Madame said proudly.

'Jack will be really sorry to have missed this feast!' Kaitlynn said bleakly. 'That dessert is his favourite dish in the world. God, I am so worried about him.' Tears rolled down her cheeks.

'I'm sure he's fine,' Roy said, and immediately realized how lame that must sound to her. It sounded pretty lame to him.

'This is not like Jack,' she said. 'Something's happened. I just hope to God he's OK.'

'Should we ask the witch to keep some food for him, Roy?' Cleo asked, in a shifty whisper.

Roy looked at his watch. It was now nearly 9 p.m. Whatever was delaying Jack, he was probably going nuts trying to contact them and not getting through. Although he felt shattered from the long drive, he knew he owed it to Jack – and to Kaitlynn – to keep trying.

The woman agreed, reluctantly, to leave out some bread and cheese and cold meats. Then, turning down her offer of coffee, the four of them thanked her for the meal, and left the table. At some point – Roy had not noticed when – the Vicomte had wheeled himself out of the room.

As they reached the bottom of the staircase, Kaitlynn hurried on up to check on Noah, who had dropped off to sleep quickly after having his supper earlier. Roy turned to Cleo. 'I'm just going to give it one more go. I'll try to start the car again. If not, I'll walk down the drive until I get a signal – sounds like the rain has stopped.'

'You look tired out, my love. Come to bed, you can't do anything more tonight.'

'I've got to keep trying,' he said, quietly, so Kaitlynn wouldn't hear. 'You've seen how upset that poor girl is, and I'm worried too. Just give me ten minutes – one last try, OK?'

Reluctantly, she said, 'Go for it.'

'I'll see you upstairs as soon as I can.' He kissed her, then walked across to the front door. Now that the rain had stopped, he would take a look under the bonnet and see if he could fix the problem. Just possibly a battery lead had been shaken off from the bumpy drive up here, although he thought that was unlikely. But surely in such a remote place as this, the owners would have a charger, or at least some jump leads?

If he couldn't fix it, he'd have a look in some of the outbuildings – there must be garages here for their cars and lawnmowers. One of them would have a charger or leads, surely? If not, he decided he would walk down the drive until he got a signal on the phone.

The two cats, with the eerie yellow eyes, that he had seen outside the front door earlier when they'd arrived, were sitting either side of the door again, this time on the inside. They looked like they were guarding it.

Roy approached the door warily, half expecting them to spring at him at any second. But they did not move. They just glared in silence. Behind him, he suddenly heard a panting and scraping sound.

He turned and saw the elderly dog pulling itself along on its front legs, dragging its hind legs behind. Both cats shot off across the hall as he pulled the heavy door open. The dog hauled itself out and passed him, bumping down the steps, then went off into the darkness, scrunching along the gravel. The poor bloody thing was clearly very ill, he thought. Much as he loved animals, shouldn't it have been put down by a vet?

He stepped out. Then frowned, switching on his phone torch. He could see the circular carriage drive, with the lake and broken statue of the cherub beyond. But he couldn't see their Citroën.

It had gone.

12

Roy did a double-take. He shone his torch around. A near full moon was breaking through ragged clouds, sending an eerie glow, enough to see the driveway was empty. For a moment he wondered, had he come out of the same door as before?

Of course he had.

Someone had moved the Citroën whilst they had been eating. But who? He frowned. So far as he was aware there was only Madame here, with her husband, the Vicomte, in a wheel-chair. One of them must have moved it. Where to? Was that why her husband had left the dining room, to very kindly call a garage out? Had he been wrong about their hosts? Had the old man pulled a favour with a local garage and arranged a breakdown truck to come out, after hours, to take the car away and bring it back tomorrow, fixed?

It seemed unlikely, yet this whole strange place was full of surprises. Could it be that their hosts were trying to make amends for Madame having been so rude to them when they first arrived?

The more he thought about it, the more he thought that must be what had happened. But, he worried, if they decided to leave in the morning, when would the car be back?

He turned and looked at the front door, as if he was going to find an answer there. But all he saw were the eyes of the two sinister cats, who had returned and were staring at him. Yellow eyes brighter than before. Was that humour in their faces? Were they mocking him?

Although he was on holiday, for a moment he switched back to being a detective. In all his experience, the most obvious answer was likely to be the correct one. And the most obvious answer right now was that Madame or her husband had called out a breakdown service and they'd towed the car off to fix it in the morning.

But if that was the case, why hadn't they told him? It made no sense. Then again, they were a pretty weird couple. Was it all part of the service? A nice little surprise? Or, as he had wondered, to make amends?

Should he believe that?

So why did he have doubts, he wondered?

Deciding to find his hosts and ask them, he hurried back inside. Only to find, to his astonishment, that the hall was in pitch darkness. All the lights had been switched off.

Charming, he thought. Without looking for a switch, he used the beam of his torch – the battery marker now on red, 18 per cent left – to guide him to the dining room. There he crossed to the door from which Madame had carried their platters of food. He went in and shone the feeble beam around a large, spotless kitchen. Their hosts had evidently gone to bed – wherever in this vast place their private living area was.

Go to bed, Roy, you're on holiday. You're meant to be taking time off, relaxing. Jack will be fine, the holiday voice inside his head told him. *He'll rock up with a perfectly good reason for being so late. All will become clear in the morning!*

But what if something's happened to Jack and he needs to get in touch urgently? the professional voice said. *You won't sleep tonight until you've done every single damned thing you can to contact him.*

And he knew he had to get a phone signal. Whatever it took.

13

Ignoring the staring cats, Roy let himself back out of the front door and instantly gagged at the awful stink of a dog poo at the bottom of the steps. Using his torch sparingly, the battery steadily ticking down – 17 per cent now – he made his way around the circular driveway, until he found the tree-lined avenue he'd driven up some five hours earlier. The air felt fresher, clearer, with the heady smell of wet grass and leaves.

He stopped, turned off Bluetooth and Wi-Fi on his phone and switched it to low-power mode.

A crackle of feathers right above him startled him, as something flew off into the night. An owl?

He walked fast, occasionally switching on the torch and using the moonlight for guidance, checking for a signal every few minutes. It took a full twenty minutes before he reached the deserted road at the bottom of the drive.

Still no signal.

Then he froze. The sound of something trampling through the undergrowth in the woods to his left. A grunting noise. A snort. Another, closer. He swung the light at it and saw a pair of small, yellow eyes. Staring at him from a huge, hairy head.

A wild boar. Stationary, watching him. He had read, somewhere, about these creatures. How dangerous they were, that they could charge and kill you. He stood his ground, holding the beam steady on its beady eyes. More boldly than he felt, he shouted at it, 'Make my day, punk!' and took a step towards it. Followed by another. 'COME ON, BIG BOY, MAKE MY BLOODY DAY!'

With a wheezy snort it turned and trotted off into the forest.

When he was sure he was out of danger, Roy rebooted the phone, in case it had a glitch. But after it finally came back to life, it still showed no signal. He set off along the road, turning right, retracing the way they had come earlier today, all the time listening out for any more of these creatures.

The darkness of the forest on either side pressed in on him, eerily. But he put it out of his mind, comforting himself with the words he'd

63

always loved and had used as a mantra whenever he was in a scary situation: *Yea, though I may walk alone through the shadow of the Valley of Death, I will fear no evil . . . for I am the meanest son-of-a-bitch in the valley.*

After another twenty minutes he stopped and again checked his phone.

Two bars!

Finally, a proper signal.

First, he checked his messages. There was only one new one, from his mate Glenn Branson, wishing him a happy holiday and telling him not to worry about work.

Nothing from Jack. No phone message or email.

Why not?

He called Jack's number. It rang. Once, twice, three times.

Come on, buddy, answer!

Ten rings and then, 'Hi, this is Detective Sergeant Jack Alexander. If your call is urgent, please call the Incident Room number at the end of this message. Otherwise please leave me a voicemail.'

'Jack, this is Roy. Where are you? We're at the chateau and we're all concerned as we haven't heard from you. Call me as soon as you can.'

He ended the call and waited for several

minutes in the hope Jack would pick this up. Then another five minutes. He saw lights in the distance. Heard the sound of an engine. Getting closer, the lights brighter. He stepped into the edge of the woods and moments later a small car, travelling recklessly fast, music blaring from a boom box, shot past. Then silence and darkness again.

Now he was even more worried about Jack. Why no message? No word? This was just not like him. He decided to call Glenn to see if he had heard anything from him.

The DI answered almost immediately and good-humouredly. 'You're meant to be on holiday, boss. Hope this isn't about work?'

'Well, not exactly.'

'Which means it is about work. We're missing you but not missing you, so relax – chillax!'

'Haha! I'm calling about Jack.'

'Yeah? Isn't he on holiday with you?'

'That's the point, matey. He's meant to be, but he's gone AWOL – you haven't heard from him, have you?'

'AWOL? Missing? What do you mean? He was going to Paris to meet with detectives there and then coming on to join you, I thought. I'm not expecting to hear from him.'

'He should have been here at midday and he hasn't showed up.'

'Roy, you know what Jack's like, he's a rottweiler. If he gets the bit between his teeth, he's on it. He's like all of us – it's why our marriages fall apart – we get caught up in the chase and forget everything else. We put locking up the bad guys ahead of looking after our loved ones.'

For a moment, Roy didn't respond. Glenn had a point. Roy's own first marriage, to Sandy, had gone south because of his dedication to his work. And so had Glenn's marriage to his wife, Ari. Being a good homicide detective could easily consume your life.

Which was why Roy had been so set on making this a proper holiday, quality time with his family – and the chateau, with its remoteness and privacy and no other guests, had seemed the ideal place for this. Perhaps in the morning, with the sun shining, it would turn out to be the paradise that he and Cleo had so much hoped for. Certainly, from the messages he had read from the celebrities and other guests who had visited over the years, it seemed the place had much to offer – even if it hadn't been immediately apparent.

But something nagged at him. A speck of worry that was growing larger with every passing moment. Gnawing at him. The same worry that he had when he sensed something wrong on a case he was trying to solve. When things didn't quite add up.

Like now.

The chateau not being what it had seemed from its online pictures. The mystery of Jack's absence. The vanished car.

And he was still puzzling over the photograph, on the drawing-room wall, of the stocky man with the wild woman on his arm. Where did he know him from?

And why did he have the feeling he recognized Madame?

Ending the call, he checked the time. It was now 10.45 p.m. He retraced his steps slowly, again checking his phone every few minutes. Still two bars of the signal, 15 per cent battery. Then one bar. And 14 per cent battery.

As he entered the gates, and traipsed back up the drive towards the chateau, the final bar disappeared. No signal now. And just a meagre 13 per cent left on the battery. Above him, the sky was clearing, the clouds thinning out and the moon giving him enough light to walk without needing the torch. It looked like tomorrow really would be a fine day.

Suddenly he froze.

A faint, distant, piercing scream cut through the silence of the night.

A fox taking a rabbit?

That was a sound he heard frequently, in the early hours, back at their country cottage in Sussex. The terrible, pitiful, wailing sound of a dying rabbit that went on and on for several seconds. But this was different.

This had sounded human.

He quickened his pace, breaking into a run, feeling sudden, deep fear. Cleo, Kaitlynn, Bruno and Noah were all alone, with just their two weird hosts. Had he imagined the sound?

No.

He heard it again. Longer. A cry for help. Then silence.

Jesus, what was happening?

He was now sprinting, perspiring, and wishing he hadn't drunk any wine at all. As he reached the circular driveway in front of the chateau, he stopped and stood still. Listening again, his heart thudding. Utter silence. The house was in pitch darkness. Not a light on anywhere. He looked up towards the tower, which was just a silhouette. No light on there at all, either.

Had Cleo gone to bed? It was unlike her. She would normally leave a light on – but the lights in that room were so feeble, maybe he couldn't see anything from here?

Then he heard a sound that chilled every cell in his body.

BLOOOP.

It came from the lake in the middle of the drive. Moments later, he heard it again.

BLOOOP.

He shone his torch on the surface, just in time to see several large bubbles burst on the surface.

BLOOOP.

And he saw dark, shimmering, disturbed water.

BLOOOP.

As if something had been submerged.

Something large.

He ran to the lake's edge and shone his torch directly on the water, just as a huge fish rose, breaking the surface, taking something. He saw an ugly, shiny, almost prehistoric head. A massive pike.

The thing seemed to be staring straight at him.

BLOOOP. It vanished, leaving a huge ripple.

Just behind him, from the chateau, he heard another scream.

And this time, he recognized Cleo's voice.

For sure.

14

Roy raced over to the porch, panic-stricken, and up the steps. He turned the brass handle and pushed the heavy front door open, the hall still in darkness.

'Cleo?' he bellowed. 'CLEO?'

He switched on the phone torch and hurried towards the staircase. Shadows jumped out at him. As if every suit of armour was moving, closing in on him. He stopped halfway and bellowed again, 'CLEOOOOOO?'

A split second later something slammed, painfully hard, into the back of his head, sending him crashing forward onto the flagstone floor. For some moments, instead of the beam of his torch, he saw shooting stars. It felt as his skull had been cracked open.

As he lay there, dazed, his brain muzzy, his phone was several feet in front of him, the torch still lit. A heavy door slammed somewhere behind him. Then he heard the clank of a key turning in a lock. The front door?

He stayed where he was, his head pounding with pain, his ears pounding with the drumbeat of his heart and the roaring of his blood.

Motionless.

Waiting.

Waiting for his attacker to make the next move.

And wondering, terrified, why Cleo had screamed.

He heard nothing. No movement. Who had hit him? Was the person standing behind him, waiting to see if he was dead or not? Ready to strike again?

Thinking more clearly with every second, he took several deep breaths, as silently as he could. Bracing himself, he lunged forward, grabbing the phone as he did so. Lurching to his feet, he swung the beam around, crouching, ready for anything that came at him.

Only shadows moved. All he could see were suits of armour, and the front door, closed. For an instant, he again imagined rows of faces behind the visors, all staring at him.

His heart was hammering like it was a crazed wild animal trying to punch its way out of his chest. His ears were popping. He flashed the beam all around. At the walls, the door, back at the suits of armour.

Who – what – had hit him?

He spun round again, shining the beam through a full 360 degrees. Nothing. No one. He touched the back of his skull and felt something wet. Blood? He had not imagined it.

Someone had very definitely hit him.

Who? Where was his attacker?

His brain raced, trying to make sense of what had happened. And why the darkness? Had lightning caused a power outage?

Then the beam caught a shape on the floor – a large object. Walking closer, warily, Roy saw what it was. A huge, stuffed wild boar head, mounted on a plinth, and lying at a drunken angle. He shone the light high up, and saw a gap between all the mounted animal heads; just a bare hook on the wall.

It had fallen off the wall. But how the hell could it have fallen?

Had someone pulled it down and thrown it at him?

Or had it simply fallen by chance and struck him?

His confused mind wondered whether it was one of the suits of armour.

Oh yeah, sure, an empty suit of armour reaches up, pulls a boar's head off the wall and throws it at me. Really?

Maybe the thunder that had shaken the house earlier somehow loosened the head and it had tumbled off the wall?

Still crouched, still turning round and round every few seconds, in case someone was creeping up behind him, he switched off his torch and moved to the bottom of the staircase. Peered up into the darkness. No sign of movement. He spun and looked behind him. Nothing. He switched the beam on for a few seconds then off again.

He ran up the steps to the landing and crashed, painfully, into something heavy and solid. The bloody stuffed stag! He switched the torch on and shone the light along the corridor. Nothing. He turned and shone it back down the stairs. No one there. Not that he could see, anyhow.

Goosebumps pricked the nape of his neck, as he walked slowly along and stopped at Bruno's door. He glanced over his shoulder once again, then opened it and peered in.

The room was empty.

Where was Bruno?

He walked further along, stopping every few moments to check behind him. Each time he saw nothing but darkness and shadows. He reached Kaitlynn's door. Again, after checking behind him, he opened it and shone his torch in.

On an empty room. And empty cot.

Oh Jesus.

It felt like an unseen hand was clamped around his throat, crushing it so tight he could barely breathe.

Where were they?

Then he heard another scream. Faint. Where was it coming from?

'Royyyyyyyyyyy!'

15

Through his pain, ravenous hunger and desperate thirst, Jack Alexander heard the distinct sound of a woman screaming, somewhere way above him. Too faint for him to make out who it was. Kaitlynn? Oh my God, what were these monsters – whoever they were – doing to her? To all of them? What was this madhouse they'd stumbled into? Who were the crazies here?

Feeling so bloody helpless, he tried desperately to think back, for any clues. All he could recall was arriving at lunchtime in a happy mood. He'd been looking forward to seeing Kaitlynn and to a holiday – thanks to Roy and Cleo's kindness – in a glorious chateau. At least, it had looked that way in the photos online – but a bit less so in the pelting rain as he had driven up. He was also looking forward to spending a week with Roy Grace, his boss.

Dating the Graces' nanny had given him this unique chance to spend an entire week on holiday with the Detective Superintendent. He could learn a lot from him, which might help his promotion prospects, he thought – and besides, he really liked him.

He recalled being surprised not to see any other cars parked outside the chateau. The unfriendly woman greeting him at the door, and a mangy dog hauling itself around on its front legs. Then something hit him. The next thing he knew, he was down here.

Nothing made sense. It was as if he was dreaming. But the pain in his head and arms was real enough. Too damned real.

Then he heard the scream again.

His wrists were agony, the bonds cutting in, as sharp as razor blades; every movement gave him burning pain. He sensed blood trickling down his arms. All the same, that scream made him try again to break free. Flexing his toes, he launched himself backwards, his cry of agony stifled by the tape around his mouth as he tried again. Then again.

And finally felt movement. Hope rose.

Whatever he was shackled to was definitely looser than it had been. Again, clenching his teeth against the pain, he sprang backwards as hard as he could. And this time he very definitely felt movement. Something was loosening on the wall.

Tears of pain stinging his eyes, he took another very deep breath and launched himself backwards once more. Suddenly, catching him out, there was no longer any resistance. His bound wrists pulled whatever they were shackled to out of the wall. It came away with a loud crack, as he fell backwards, painfully, onto the hard floor.

He lay for some moments in the darkness, winded, collecting his thoughts, his hands still tightly bound and attached to something heavy. He brought it to his face. It felt like a metal hoop.

Sneezing from the dust, he knelt and brought his wrists to his face, rubbing them against his cheek to try to figure out what the bindings were. They felt like cable ties, made from plastic as hard as steel. Giving up, he stumbled to his feet and stood, confused, in the pitch darkness, swaying unsteadily. His watch was meant to be luminous, but he couldn't see the hands. Maybe he'd been in the dark too long.

Then he used his fingers to work away at the tape over his lips and chin. It took him several anxious minutes before, finally and gratefully, he was able to uncover his mouth.

'Hello?' he said to the man and woman he had seen in here. 'Hello? *Bonjour?*'

Nothing.

He stumbled around in the darkness, thinking this was what it must be like to be blind. Where was the door? Was there some sharp edge down here he could rub the cable tie against? Then he banged into something hard, flat, cold and damp. A wall.

Just keep moving in one direction and I'll come to a door, he thought.

Keeping his right elbow against the wall, he began inching along. Suddenly, after only a few paces, he felt a cold draught. Then wood on his hand.

A door!

Open, please God.

Using both hands now, he felt the coarse surface, wincing as a painful splinter dug into his skin. Then a square, metal lock. And the handle.

His heart pounding, he turned the handle. Pulled. Pushed. Pulled again as hard as he could, then pushed once more. But the door did not move. It was locked.

Shit, shit, shit.

Tempted to start pounding with his fists, he thought better of it. Stealth. Keep quiet and his captors would not know he was free. That gave him one small edge over them, even though his wrists were still bound together. He tried to cut through the tie using the edge of the lock, but it wasn't sharp enough.

What else was here? Another door? Window? Air vent?

He smelled piss, and realized it was his own, from some time ago – he had no idea how long – when he'd finally relieved himself.

He carried on, keeping the back of his hand against the wall, feeling his way around his prison. Desperate to get out, to find Kaitlynn – and to find out just what the hell was going on here. Then, suddenly, his foot struck something hard, sending him hurtling forward onto the floor.

He lay for some moments, winded and bruised. Then, as he hauled himself back up, his face brushed against something soft and firm. Something covered in fabric. A trouser leg? It moved away. An instant later, something crashed into his face with such force it knocked him over onto his back.

As he lay on the ground, the taste of blood in his mouth, checking if he had lost a tooth – and confirming it with his tongue – he realized he had been kicked in the face. 'Hey!' he called out, aware his voice sounded strange, slurred, as if his jaw was broken. 'I am your friend – *ami!*'

He climbed back, unsteadily, onto his feet.

'Englishhh!' he slurred. 'I'm an English police officer. *Je suis* police, *gendarme*! Friend! *Ami!*'

He inched his way back to the wall, grateful when he finally touched it, and stood there, not daring to get too close to whoever had kicked him. 'Police!' he said again, his voice drowning out the sound of the door opening a short distance away. '*Ami!* Friend!'

Making his way along, he touched the leg again. This time it did not flinch. 'Do you speak English? *Parlez-vous Anglais?* Raise your right leg if you do!'

An instant later, he was startled by a powerful beam of light from behind him. For a moment, it lit up an elderly man, with messy hair and terror in his eyes, his mouth and chin covered in duct tape. Beside him was a similarly gagged woman, maybe in her late sixties, also chained to the wall by her wrists.

Then, just as Jack turned his head, he felt a violent blow. He fell sideways, unconscious, to the floor.

16

'Royyyyyyyyyyy!'

The sound pierced Roy Grace's heart.

He heard her again. She was shouting something, a warning. It sounded like, 'Royyyyy! Get away, run! They're going to kill you!'

He realized that he had never, in the years he had been with Cleo, heard her scream before – apart from one time when she'd found a huge spider in the shower tray. The scream had definitely come from above.

Roy sprinted the short distance along the corridor to the tower steps and climbed them as fast as he could, hauling himself by the handrail. In the beam of his torch, as he passed the fuse box, he noticed the trip handle was up.

Hadn't it been down when he'd come up here earlier? The lightning must have tripped it, which would explain the darkness, he thought, as he continued climbing, giddily, round and round. At last, breathless, his lungs feeling like they were on fire, he reached the tiny landing at the top. The closed oak door of their room was in front of him.

He tried the handle, but it was locked. He pounded on the door, yelling, 'Cleo? Cleo?'

'Roy?' The voice from the other side sounded scared. Really scared.

'Can you open the door, darling?' he shouted.

'We're locked in,' she called back.

'Who's with you?'

'Bruno, Noah and Kaitlynn.' She sounded calm, despite the fear in her voice.

He tried again, frantically, to open the door, kicking hard at the lock, a door's weak point, with all his strength. But it did not budge. Without the key it was going to need a bosher or a sledge-hammer. All the same, he kicked again, with no success, desperately wishing he had heavy boots on, instead of his trainers.

'Roy!' Cleo called, louder now. 'Don't worry about us, get away! Run! Get the police!'

Jesus. 'What the hell's happening?' he shouted.

'Roy, darling, get out of here, get away, it's you they want!'

'What do you mean?' he shouted back.

'They're crazy, Roy, be careful, be careful. It's you they want.'

'Me? What do you mean, Cleo? What do they want from me? Who do you mean?'

What madhouse had they come to?

'I don't know; I don't know who the hell they are. They're crazy.'

He heard Noah crying.

Was this a bad dream?

If only.

What the hell to do? Somehow get out of here and go for help. His brain raced, spinning, trying to get a grip. Thinking fast. There were windows downstairs and patio doors leading out to a terrace at the rear. If he went down, he would be invisible in the darkness. Make a dash for the patio doors, smash through them and run?

Run how far? He tried to remember the last town they had driven through – it must have been a good ten miles or more away. If he could get to the road, perhaps he could flag down a passing car? Even though he'd only seen one vehicle in the half-hour or so he'd been there before, there must be others using that road. Perhaps holidaymakers like themselves? It seemed at this moment to be his best shot.

Just 9 per cent left on his phone battery.

'I'll be back as quickly as I can, darling!' he shouted.

'Please be careful! Just get away from here!' she urged. 'You *must* get away!'

'I love you,' he said. 'I'll be back with help.'

With his heart in his mouth, he made his way back down the spiral staircase, silently, stealthily, guided by the beam of the phone torch. He stopped when he reached the landing beneath the fuse box. Stared at the handle. It was a big, old-fashioned handle, like a lever. Like the one in his parents' house. Could a lightning strike have tripped it? No. A strike might have taken the power out by causing a short. But it wouldn't have lifted this heavy handle.

Someone, he realized with a chill, had done that deliberately.

He studied it for some moments, looking at the thick cable that ran down from it into the floor, and the other two thinner cables hanging loose. For a moment he was tempted to reach up and pull the handle down, which might bring the lights back on.

But then what? Back in England he could have called for back-up. He would have had a dozen officers, including an Armed Response Unit, on the scene in minutes. But not here, in deep countryside in a foreign land. In the middle of sodding nowhere.

Right now he was safer under the cover of darkness. Stealth. The element of surprise on his side. He checked his pockets for loose change, or anything else that might clink or jangle and give him away. Removing a handful of coins, he laid them on the step. He thought about taking off his shoes to prevent any squeak from his rubber soles – then decided that running barefoot along the road wasn't a clever idea. He switched off the torch and, on tiptoe, carried on down the steps until he felt the landing.

Still on tiptoe, and fearful of a creaking floorboard giving him away, he moved along, feeling the wall to his left and then the first door – to Kaitlynn's room. Then the door to Bruno's room. He carried on, slowly, slowly, slowly. Silently. Until he felt the head of the stag. He edged around it and felt the banister post at the top of the staircase. Holding his breath, he began to descend into the pitch darkness. One slow, delicate step at a time. Until he reached the bottom.

He paused, remembering something he had been taught many years ago, and opened his mouth. You could hear better with your mouth open.

He listened. Silence. Trying to locate himself. He knew that over to his left would be the front door, some distance across the hallway. To his right, the patio doors and windows either side. He could see them in the faint glow through the windows from the moonlight outside.

Breathing as quietly as he could, he quickened his pace, tiptoeing towards them. Closer and closer. As he neared, he could see the glass doors even more clearly.

He was unaware that he was being watched, in sharp detail, through the green of night-vision goggles.

Suddenly, yellow eyes peered at him out of the darkness. A cat. Ignoring it, Roy reached the patio doors, ready to try the handles and, if they were locked, to dive head first through them.

As he peered out into the moonlit darkness, a stag's head, brightly lit from beneath, reared up and darted at the glass, its antlers rattling the panes, startling the hell out of him.

An instant later there was a brilliant flash of light behind him, followed by a loud bang. Then another. Another.

BANG BANG BANG.

He spun round in shock. Smelled gunpowder. And saw a firecracker jumping around the floor.

BANG BANG BANG.

For an instant he froze.

The firecracker fizzled out into silence.

A hooded head, with tiny eye slits, lit from below like the stag's head, appeared in the window. Pointing a shotgun straight at him.

It was joined by a voice. Nasty, sinister,

mocking. A Scouse accent, booming in the echoing silence. 'Hello, Roy! So nice to see you again! Are you enjoying your cosy little family holiday? I do hope so! Remember me?'

He knew that voice. From somewhere.

'Thought you were meant to be a sharp detective. But you didn't recognize me in the wheelchair, did you? Nor did you recognize Monica who greeted you when you arrived.'

Monica? Who the hell was Monica?

'She's changed a bit, my old pal, in the past fifteen years, with the help of a wig, make-up and glasses. But hey, haven't we all? Fooled you so easily – you must be slipping in your old age! But here's the thing, Detective Superintendent – my, how you've been promoted in the years since we met – you were just a humble Detective *Sergeant*, then. You and I have a score to settle. All those years in the *big house*. You thought that was the end of me and Monica, didn't you? Did you count on us being out so soon for good behaviour? I don't think so.'

And suddenly, Roy did remember. Those eyebrows.

'I spent all that time in my prison cell working out my revenge, Roy. Ever tried sleeping on a prison pillow, Roy? Rock hard they are. Like sleeping on a six-inch-thick breeze block. So I didn't sleep much, see. Just lay there every night, thinking, planning, dreaming. Dreaming of the day I would make you pay. And now, *voilà*! With what I've got in mind, you and your family are all going to wish you were dead.'

17

The man's voice.

The woman's face. Her eyebrows.

Snapping on his phone light again, Roy ran back towards the drawing room across the hall from the dining room. The room that was hung with photographs of past guests, including all the many famous names. And there, beneath the photographs of Peter Sellers and the footballer George Best, was one of a thuggish man in his fifties. He had almost no neck, short gelled hair and he stood with his arm around the woman with the thick eyebrows. A scrawled message beneath – 'What a gem we've discovered!' – followed by the date.

With a chill, he now knew for sure who they both were – how had he missed it earlier? Probably too struck by the other famous faces.

And he knew that distinctive voice.

He remembered all too clearly where he had last heard it. In Courtroom One of the Central

Criminal Court of England and Wales – the Old Bailey.

And Cleo had been right when she said she did not believe French was the woman's first language. It wasn't – it was English. And she wasn't *Monique*, she was *Monica*.

He looked at the date. They must have stayed here just four months ago.

Curtis Esmonde.

One of the nastiest villains he'd locked up in twenty years of being a copper. Esmonde's speciality, together with his evil sidekick, Monica Stokes, had been terrorizing helpless elderly people in their homes. They would torture them to get their pin numbers and clear out their bank accounts, sometimes even cutting off fingers to get their rings. If any resisted, they would beat them unconscious.

Staring at the image, Roy remembered the case so well. And, of course, he would. It had been his detective work that had led to their arrest, and which had caught the eye of his then Chief Constable, leading to his fast-track promotion. First to Detective Inspector and soon after to Detective Chief Inspector and his move to the Major Crime Team.

He remembered taking the witness stand in the scary grandeur of the Old Bailey, as a young

DS. He had told the judge that in all his six years as a police officer, Esmonde was the vilest piece of low-life he had ever met. As was his partner, Monica Stokes. They'd seen themselves as a modern-day Bonnie and Clyde, but in reality they were nothing more than a pair of cold-blooded scumbags.

How on earth were they here now?

How *could* they be here?

There was a window to his left. Snapping off the torch, he ran over to it. But as he reached it, a powerful beam shone in, dazzling him. Something hard and metallic tapped on the windowpane. He could just make out the twin muzzles of a double-barrelled shotgun. He threw himself down below the sill an instant before there was a massive explosion, followed a moment later by another, as glass showered down on him.

Jesus.

Crouching low, phone off, he ran back in the direction of the door, misjudged it and crashed painfully into the wall. Mocking laughter seemed to echo all around. He dived for the floor again as two more shots rang out and chippings of plaster fell onto him and around him.

A million questions flashed through his brain. But he had only one purpose right at this second – to somehow stay alive and get his family to safety.

Curtis Esmonde's voice boomed out at him. 'So nice to be here with you, Roy. Dead nice! Having a dead nice holiday, are you? Remember what you called me in court when you were giving evidence? What you told the jury? And that bitch of a judge, what was her name? You said I was vermin; you likened me to a scavenging sewer rat. Well, who's the rat now? The rat trapped in a maze, eh? We did leave you a clue with the photograph on the wall, but you must have missed it, Roy. Tut tut, and I thought you were supposed to be such a sharp detective.'

But Roy was barely listening. An idea was forming. A desperate plan. If he could stay alive long enough.

He rolled over, feeling the edge of the door frame, and crawled on all fours through into the hall. Two more shots rang out in rapid succession. Something zinged by his right ear. Fleetingly, snapping on his torch, he saw the nearest suit of armour to his left. It had a large shield. He turned the torch off and ducked behind the armour, crouching as low as he could.

He tried to free the shield, but it felt as if it was welded to the steel hand. Still crouched, he moved across the hall, dragging the suit of armour behind him for protection. Shit, it was heavy. Another two shots. Shotgun pellets pinged off the armour and something stung his left arm, painfully. He'd been hit.

From the time it had taken Esmonde to fire again, Roy guessed – and hoped – this wasn't a pump-action gun; that the bastard was having to break the barrel open to reload fresh cartridges. Giving him a precious few seconds.

Switching on the torch again – 5 per cent charge remaining – and breaking into a run, he dragged the suit of armour behind him to the doorway through into the windowless dining room. Leaving it there, he sprinted across the room to the far door, through which Madame had brought the food on the large silver trays. And into the kitchen again.

He shone the beam around wildly. Desperately hoping to see what he was looking for. The two objects he needed to stay alive. Suddenly he spotted the first one – a block of kitchen knives on a work surface close to the huge butler's sink. He grabbed the largest knife, a thick, serrated one, and pulled it out. Then, turning round, he saw one of the large silver trays, laden with plates and wine glasses, sitting on a long wooden table.

He lifted the tray up, hurling the contents

93

onto the floor with a deafening crash of breaking glass and crockery. 'Apologies, Madame,' he murmured. 'Send me the bill.' He switched his torch off, then went back to the doorway and, by memory, through the windowless dining room to the doorway to the hall.

Stopping in the entrance, he gripped the handle of the knife in his teeth and held the tray out like a shield with his left hand. With his right hand he shoved the suit of armour hard, sending it toppling over with a loud crash.

At the same moment, he switched on the beam again, shining it on his own face. Then he held up the tray and stepped back as two more shots rang out in quick succession, a volley of pellets pinging off the tray.

With the torch still on, knife gripped tightly in his teeth, he sprinted across the hall, ignoring the voice that was taunting him. He reached the bottom of the stairs and flashed the torch beam up at the huge stuffed stag on the first landing.

'This is such fun, Roy!' he heard. 'Like shooting fish in a barrel! Or since you prefer rodents, it's just like playing whack-a-mole! Or maybe it's *voles* that are rodents, but hey, old pal, we're not going to split hairs, are we, Roy?

'And just imagine what fun I'm going to have with your beautiful wife and that very sexy nanny of yours after I've shot your head off. And I wonder how high that kid and that stupid little baby of yours will bounce when I chuck them out of the top of the tower. Who will bounce higher – the boy or the baby? How high? Four feet? Want to have a bet with me? Four feet, six feet or just three? Or no bounce at all, just splat! Oh, sorry, I forgot – you won't be around to pay out.'

18

Roy's brain ripped through his few options. The stairs were a big gamble, and if he got this wrong, he would be trapped. A sitting target. But right now they seemed to be his only real chance. It was a dangerous gamble. He had to make it work.

Two more shots fired. Pellets pinged off the tray and off the banisters as he sprinted up the stairs to the landing, turning off his torch again at the top. He leaned the silver tray against the wall, then squeezed into the gap behind the massive stag as another two shots fired. Pellets thudded into the wood panelling above him. Ignoring them, he pushed as hard as he could with his hand.

Shit, it was heavy.

For a moment he wondered if he had misjudged his own strength. The bloody thing would not move.

Come on, come on, come on.

Wedging his back against the wall, he lifted his feet off the ground, one at a time, and pressed them against the belly of the solid animal. Its weight supported him. But his back was starting to slip down the wall. He couldn't stay here for long. *But he had to stay long enough.*

Pushing with every ounce of strength he had, he felt the stag finally budge, a few inches.

'Not a smart move, Roy Grace,' Esmonde's voice called out. 'No way down from there! Monica, you remember all those vile names he called you in court – do the honours, *ma chérie*!'

Yes, Roy thought, *do the honours!* He rapped the knife hard against the wood panelling of the wall, deliberately making as loud a noise as he could. Moments later he heard movement in the darkness below him.

He heard a female voice, with a mocking French accent, call out, 'It will be my pleasure, *mon chéri*!'

He rapped the knife again and seconds later heard footsteps coming up the stairs. Slowly. Steadily. Getting closer. Nearer.

Taking a deep breath, after years of doing leg-presses in the gym he kicked both legs out, sending the stag toppling over the top step of the landing and tumbling down. Down. Down.

THUMP . . . THUMP . . . THUMP . . .

Then a terrible scream and a crashing noise.

There was a moment of complete silence.

Followed by a horrible gurgling.

He snapped on the torch and looked down. And saw the stag lying on its side with a woman trapped beneath it. Before he switched the torch off again, he saw that one of the antlers had pierced her neck.

Esmonde shouted. 'Monica! Monica! Are you OK?'

Without waiting, grabbing the tray and again gripping the knife tightly in his teeth, Roy sprinted along the landing. He climbed as fast as he could up the spiral steps of the tower, switching on the torch again as he went. He raced on round and up, his chest heaving, gasping for breath and his whole body pounding, until he stopped at what he guessed to be one spiral turn below the landing where the fuse box was.

3 per cent battery.

Please last. Please, he willed it.

2 per cent.

Then, from down below, he heard Esmonde's voice again, now an awful scream. 'Monica, oh my God, Monica! MONICA! Oh Jesus, oh no!'

Then an instant of silence before Roy heard him again.

'You're not going to get away from me up there, you evil bastard, Roy!' Esmonde's voice was full of bitter anger. 'You've put yourself into a trap – a rat trap! Tut tut, and I thought you were smart. Not too smart now, are you? I'm coming for you! I've got two very special cartridges with nice heavy shot for bringing down wild boars. Just right for shooting a pig!'

As silently as he could, aware he was taking the gamble of his life, Roy placed the tray down on a step below him. To his relief, the stone step was just wide enough for the tray to balance. Then he hurried on up to the landing.

He shone the light on the two-inch-thick insulated cable running from the base of the fuse box and down the wall, held by old, rusty metal clips all the way to the floor. Here, it disappeared into a small hole in the wood. Roy grabbed the bottom of the cable and wrenched it free of the clips. Then he yanked it up, hard. It rose a few inches, giving him the slack he had prayed for. He began sawing through the cable with the knife.

Shit, it was as hard as steel. And making a loud grinding noise.

Down below he heard footsteps.

He kept sawing away, desperately pushing the blade with all his strength, ignoring the noise. The footsteps were approaching. Coming closer. Closer.

With one final effort, the blade cut through the cable.

Footsteps nearer still.

He had maybe thirty seconds. Desperately, gripping the bottom end of the sawn-off cable, he hacked away at the thick plastic insulation, working round until he had a good inch of bare copper wire exposed.

Roy could hear Esmonde breathing heavily. Coming closer.

Closer.

He put the cable on the metal handrail, winding the wires around it as best he could. Then he raised his arm, gripped the handle on the fuse box with his fingers and switched off the torch. He held his breath. Opened his mouth.

He could hear the footsteps and heavy breathing even more clearly now.

'I'm coming for you, Roy!' Wheezing, Esmonde called out, 'How does it feel to be a dead man walking? Good, eh? Does it feel good?'

Then he heard a *clank*, signalling that Esmonde had reached the tray. It was followed, a second later, by a loud clattering, as if he had tossed it aside and it was now tumbling down the steps.

'That your best effort to stop me?' Esmonde

shouted, wheezing even more. 'You'd better try harder than that!'

Roy heard him panting, clearly struggling to climb. Roy desperately hoped that he was using the handrail to help himself up.

Then, praying he wasn't making the most terrible mistake of his life, Roy pulled the fuse box handle down with all his strength.

Instantly the staircase lights came on. At the same time there was a fierce crackle of electricity. He held the handle down, grimly. And in the same moment he heard a terrible cry, followed by the echoing explosion of a gun discharging.

And he heard an awful, pitiful croaking sound.

'URR! URRRRRR! URRRRRRRRR!'

He waited several seconds. Then the sharp smell of burning flesh struck his nostrils.

Waving the knife, Roy took a careful step back, down and round. Then, as he took a second step, he saw Esmonde. His left hand was clamped to the rail. His feet, in fancy loafers, were doing a jig that reminded Roy of Irish dancing. His hair, which was gelled flat in the photograph downstairs, was standing on end, as if a thousand invisible strings were pulling the strands. His eyes, inside night-vision goggles, were wide open and bulging as if they were about to pop their sockets. Smoke curled out of each of his ears. His skin was visibly darkening with every second that Roy looked at him, as if he was being cooked from inside.

'Toasting your freedom, eh, Curtis?' Roy couldn't help saying as he yanked the handle back up, plunging them again into darkness. He snapped on his torch – 2 per cent power left – in time to see Esmonde topple backwards.

1 per cent.

Roy just had time to get down the few steps to where the villain lay. He checked his pulse in the remaining light, to be sure he was dead. He pulled the night-vision goggles off the man and put them on himself, just as his phone gave out.

19

In the green glow of the goggles, Roy saw wisps of smoke still curling up from Curtis Esmonde's body. Squeezing past, he grabbed the gun, broke the barrel open and ejected the spent cartridge. He rummaged in the man's jacket and found a handful of live cartridges. He pulled out two, stuck them into the barrel and closed it. He pushed the remaining cartridges into his trouser pocket.

He was pretty sure Monica was dead, but did they have a friend here? Downstairs, somewhere? In the house or out in the darkness, waiting for him?

Roy took a few seconds to study the gun, trying to remember what he had learned on firearms courses he had attended. When you closed the barrels on most shotguns, the safety catch – a lever on the top – normally engaged. He tried it one way, where it would not budge, then the other. Well-oiled, it moved smoothly, and stopped with a sturdy click.

The gun was now cocked.

Holding the weapon out in front of him, his finger on the twin triggers, he began inching his way back down the steps. Slowly, carefully, breathing as silently as he could, he went on down, able to see perfectly through the lenses. His finger kept pressure on the trigger, ready to pull it, instantly.

Reaching the landing, he looked along it and waited, for several seconds. No sign of anyone. Sweat was running down his back. If there was another villain, did they have night-vision goggles, too?

Almost certainly.

He reached the top of the stairs and saw, on the floor below, the fallen stag, with a wide pool of blood spreading steadily out close to its head. A shotgun and a pair of night-vision goggles were a short distance away. Beside them was a wig.

But no Monique – Monica.

Where was she?

Then he heard a weak moaning sound. And saw her. She was crawling across the hall, between the suits of armour, trying to get to the front door, a trail of blood running from her neck.

Several feet from the stag, her arms stretched out, she slumped down face-forward and stopped.

Watching her closely and keeping his gun trained on her, he hurried down the stairs and grabbed the shotgun. Then, looking around warily, he walked over to her. She was breathing in short, rapid bursts and appeared to be very weak. And now, without her wig, with her short, natural, spiky hair, he recognized her even more clearly.

Her eyes flicked open. 'Curt? Curt, everything OK? What happened – did you get him?' Her voice was rasping. Close to a death rattle, a horrible sound he had heard once before.

'Your lover boy's lying down, he's had a bit of a shock.'

'Curt?' she whispered.

Roy knelt beside her. 'Didn't Curt ever tell you that proverb from Confucius? *Before you seek revenge, first dig two graves. One for yourself.*'

She blinked at him, looking weaker by the second.

'You know you're not getting out of this alive, Monica – just do one good thing. Where is the key to the bedroom and where is my friend, Jack?'

She spoke slowly, her voice weakening. 'Curt's – idea. In – my pocket – keys. He – he's – in – kitchen – wine cellar. He—'

Her eyes froze open.

Her breathing stopped.

Looking carefully around again, Roy rummaged in the pockets of her denim jacket and found two large keys. He checked the woman's pulse, carefully, counting the seconds. There was nothing. Thirty seconds, then a full minute, to be sure.

She was gone.

Picking up both guns, he hurried back, past the toppled stag and up to the landing, running on pure adrenaline. He raced along and began climbing steps, holding the guns in one hand and the rail in the other. He edged past Esmonde's body, trying to ignore the stench of seared flesh, and finally, gasping for air, stood – almost sagging to his knees – outside the door to their room.

Taking a moment to calm himself and get his breath back, he shouted, 'It's me, you're all safe, I'm coming in!'

He tried the first of the two keys in the lock. To his relief, it turned. Even so, he was cautious – just in case there was a buddy of the two scumbags in there with them. Laying one gun down and gripping the other with both hands, keeping it pointed at the floor, he kicked the door wide open.

And to his immense relief – and joy – through

his goggles he saw Cleo, Bruno and Kaitlynn sitting on the bed, where Noah lay fast asleep, despite everything. They were all staring towards him, although he knew they couldn't actually see him in the darkness. Bruno seemed to be busily untying the laces of one of his trainers.

Knackered and still panting heavily, Roy spluttered, 'Are you all OK? Are any of you hurt?'

'We're fine, just shaken. Are you OK, darling?' Cleo asked, anxiously.

'I'm OK,' he replied, forgetting at that moment the stinging pain in his arm from the pellet – or pellets – that had hit him. All that mattered was that they all looked fine, that they didn't look hurt, thank God. 'I can see you all, I'm wearing night-vision goggles. You're all safe. I'm going to get you out of here.'

'Night-vision goggles – cool!' Bruno said.

'Where's Jack?' Kaitlynn asked, anxiously. 'Any word?'

'He's here. I know where he is.'

'Is he OK?'

'Yes,' he said, fibbing, desperately hoping Jack was OK, not wanting to panic her. He snapped on the safety catch, put the gun down then rushed over and threw his arms around Cleo, hugging her tight, tight, tight. Hugging her and loving her almost more than it was possible to love another human being, as a tear trickled down his cheek.

An instant later, a brilliant light shone in his face, dazzling him.

20

Freeing himself from Cleo's arms, Roy turned his head away. The light was coming from Bruno.

'Wow, those are so cool, Papa!'

'Bruno!' Cleo said sternly. 'Not at his face.'

Roy looked back and saw Bruno pointing his phone torch at the floor.

'They took our phones,' Cleo said.

'But not mine, Papa,' Bruno boasted. 'I hid it in my shoe!'

'Well done, good thinking!' Roy replied.

'I read it in an Alex Rider book!' he said proudly. 'He did that!'

'Darling, you're bleeding – your arm,' Cleo said.

'It's OK, it's nothing – I just caught it on something.'

'It's bleeding badly!' she insisted.

'We'll deal with it later. We need to find Jack.'

Roy told a reluctant Kaitlynn and Bruno to stay with Noah, and told them to lock themselves in, for their safety, just in case there was someone else here. He stood with Cleo on the landing, telling her they would walk down very slowly and he would warn her when they came to an obstacle. The door behind them opened and he saw the bright beam of Bruno's torch.

'I'm coming, too!' the boy announced firmly, as the door closed and was locked behind him.

Roy thought for a moment. Should he insist he stay up here with the nanny and Noah? He didn't want him to see the horror of the two bodies. On the other hand, his torch would be helpful to guide Cleo down these dangerous steps. 'OK,' he said, reluctantly.

He led Cleo and Bruno very slowly back down the stairs, passing the fuse box and the blackened wires around the rail. The bright beam of Bruno's phone torch briefly dazzled him as it shone on Curtis Esmonde's legs.

'Who's that?' Bruno asked.

Trying to block the boy's view, to shield him from the horror of the corpse, Roy ushered him on down. 'Oh, he's just my old mate, Curtis,' he said, matter-of-factly. 'He thought it would be nice to drop in and see us. Thought it would be a bundle of laughs.'

But Bruno, very firmly, stopped and shone the

beam towards Esmonde's face. Just in time, Roy gripped the boy's shoulders and turned him away.

'Is that the man who made us go up the tower and took Mama and Kaitlynn's phones?' Bruno asked. 'There was a horrible woman, too. They said they would kill us all if we did not obey.'

Cleo took Bruno's phone and knelt beside the body. She'd seen enough corpses in her career to know instantly when someone was dead. She turned to Roy. 'What happened?' she asked, shocked.

Roy looked at his wife, and even in the ghostly green glow saw the kindness in her face. That kindness was one of the many things that he had fallen in love with. But fury about what Curtis Esmonde and Monica Stokes had planned for him and Cleo – and the rest of his family – still raged like a furnace inside him.

'I'll tell you later.'

'What's happened to him, Roy?' she asked again, insistently, her voice trembling. 'He's got burn marks.' She frowned.

'Is he drunk, Papa?' Bruno called out.

'Yes, Bruno. He's very drunk.'

Before either could ask any more questions, Roy ushered them on down, along the landing and then down again into the hall. Cleo briefly lit up the dead woman's face with the torch beam.

'That's her,' she said, moving the beam swiftly away. 'Roy, what happened?' she asked again.

Ignoring the question, Roy led the way into the dining room, entered the kitchen, walked through a huge cold room at the far end and saw a closed door. Opening it, warning Cleo and Bruno to stay back, he went down a steep staircase into a vast wine cellar. To his left he saw a thick oak door. He tried the handle and, sure enough, it was locked. He pulled the second large, ancient key from his pocket, inserted it and twisted. Nothing happened. He tried again. Then again.

21

Jack Alexander lay on the cold stone floor, in the darkness. The inside of his head felt like it was being burned by a blowtorch. Thinking, muzzily, about Kaitlynn. What the hell was happening to her? Was she captured, too? In terror?

Somehow, he had to get out of here and find her.

Had to.

Perhaps the two old people he'd seen moments before he'd been struck on the head might know something. He urgently needed to get the tape off their mouths and talk to them.

The one thing he held on to, keeping him sane in this nightmare, was the confidence he had in his abilities. He knew he was smart. And sure as hell – whatever vicious thugs had captured him and were holding him prisoner – he was pretty sure he was smarter than they were.

So prove it, Detective Sergeant Alexander, the

voice inside his head had been saying over and over.

In his work with the Surrey and Sussex Major Crime team, he was well aware that surprise was often the key element. Surprising villains when they were least expecting it, catching them off-guard. Like dawn raids on drug dealers. Or producing digital evidence from their phones and computers that they were totally not expecting. Or finding a witness they'd not thought about. Out-thinking them was the key.

And he was going to out-think whoever that bastard was who had come in here with the torch and slugged him.

Suddenly, he heard a *clank*.

The sound of a key in the door lock.

Shit.

Clank.

The bastard was coming back. He tried to stand up, but with his hands still bound together he stumbled and fell flat on his face.

Clank.

It sounded like the key had turned.

The door was opening.

With every ounce of his strength, he managed to stand up, giddy with fury. He saw the chink of light and raced to the side of the door, flattening himself against the wall. Then he raised the heavy iron hoop high above his head.

Ready.

Ready for you, you bastard.

22

Signalling to Cleo and Bruno to stay back, Roy Grace pushed the massive, heavy door open, slowly, cautiously, and peered in.

What he saw was something out of a horror film. Two people, a man and a woman, their mouths covered with duct tape, bound by their wrists to iron hoops on a wall.

But, to his dismay, there was no sign of Jack.

He strode in and was about to call out that he was a police officer when he was aware, too late, of a shape hurtling down at him from his left. He felt a crashing blow. His head exploded into a shower of sparks. He stumbled forward, dizzily, a few steps, his legs cut off from his brain. Then the floor came rushing up, smashing his goggles against his face. The sparks inside his head flickered out.

23

Roy tried to open his eyes, and immediately closed them again against painfully dazzling light. He was totally confused. His brain felt like it was on a helter-skelter, swirling round and round, down and down.

Somewhere distant, he heard a man's voice, speaking quietly in French. *'Il se réveille!'*

He opened his eyes again, just a tiny slit, blinking hard. A blurry face that he thought, for a moment, was an angel peered down at him, part anxious, part smiling.

'Darling, thank God!' Cleo's voice, as if in a dream, sounding echoey. Another blurry figure next to hers, a woman dressed all in white, was now stooping over him as if she was studying an object in a museum.

His vision remained blurred. For some moments he wondered if he was dead.

He blinked, painfully. It felt as if a knife was digging into the base of his skull. Slowly, Cleo came into focus. Then the kindly face of the young woman beside her. A nurse, he realized.

As he looked around, he saw he was surrounded by medical gear. A drip line was taped to the back of his left hand and there was a plastic bracelet on his wrist instead of his watch. He tried to speak but no sound would come out.

The nurse said something in French. It sounded approving. He recognized one of the words, *bien*.

Cleo leaned down and kissed him on the forehead. 'Darling, welcome back.' She was crying. 'God, thank God. You're OK!'

A tear fell on his face. He reached up with his right hand to his forehead and touched what felt like a sticking plaster.

A thin man in white scrubs, with a stethoscope around his neck, suddenly appeared. For some moments he studied a bank of screens on shelves above him, displaying changing graphs and readouts, and nodded approvingly. Roy heard the words, in broken English, 'It is good, the brainwaves are normal now, his heart rate is up, his pulse is good. *Fort* – strong!'

Roy tried to sit up, but the nurse immediately held him back. '*S'il vous plaît* – please – just rest.'

Again he tried to speak, but his voice came out slurred, as if he was drunk. 'Was – was happened?'

He felt a tiny prick in his arm, then everything went dark again.

24

When Roy next opened his eyes, the light in the room had changed – it was less bright. He saw a large window over to his right, with a view out onto buildings. Dusk had fallen. He was dizzy; it felt as if an entire workshop of panel beaters was bashing away inside his skull. Someone was holding his right hand. He turned and saw Cleo sitting at his side, smiling at him.

'Hi!' he said.

'My darling, my poor brave soldier. How are you feeling?'

It took him some moments to process the question. How was he feeling? Like shit. It was all starting to come back now. Curtis Esmonde. Monica Stokes. He'd gone through the kitchen, down into the cellar and unlocked the door. Then he was here.

Wherever here was.

He heard another familiar voice. 'I'm sorry, boss. Shit, I'm so sorry.'

Unshaven, hair tangled, in jeans and a grey

Pink Floyd T-shirt, Detective Sergeant Jack Alexander smiled down at him, sheepishly. He looked tired, with hollow rings around his eyes. 'Thank God you're OK, boss – I honestly thought I'd killed you.'

'So it was you! You obviously didn't hit me hard enough!'

Jack blushed and looked even more sheepish.

'Where the hell am I?'

'You're in hospital in Nantes, darling,' Cleo said. 'You've been here overnight.'

'Overnight?'

'I'm really sorry, boss. I didn't realize it was you when you came into the cellar. I thought it was one of those bastards.'

'What about Noah, Bruno, Kaitlynn? Are they safe?' Roy asked.

'All good,' Jack told him. 'Thanks to you – less thanks to me.'

'The doctors think you should be OK to leave later today,' Cleo said. 'Depending how you're feeling. They want to do another brain scan, just to be sure.'

'Yeah, they couldn't find it last time, boss,' Jack said.

'Haha!' Roy replied, weakly. And was pleased to see Cleo grin.

'And then we go back to the chateau?' he asked.

'Happily, not,' she replied. 'It's all sealed up as a crime scene.'

'Some holiday this, eh?' Roy said.

'The local police here have been wonderful,' she said. 'They've found us a gorgeous country house hotel, with a big pool and loads of luxury. Kaitlynn is there now with Noah and Bruno.'

He was slowly starting to feel more human, but he had a raging thirst. 'Water – could I have water?' He struggled to sit up.

'I'll do it!' Cleo said. She picked up a remote and pressed a button. Immediately the back of the bed began to rise, until Roy was sitting almost upright.

Cleo held a paper cup to his lips, and he drank the cold water, gratefully.

'So, tell me,' he said, 'what happened after Jack decided to play baseball with my head?'

'God, it was terrible. We both thought he'd killed you. We freed the real Vicomte and Vicomtesse – such a sweet old couple. They're in a terrible state of shock. They tried to phone an ambulance and the police, but it turned out the phone line had been cut and the internet router smashed. Their car wouldn't start and Jack's and yours had been moved to a stable block and disabled.'

'Courtesy of my old buddies Curtis Esmonde and Monica Stokes?'

'Presumably. Jack and Bruno went off on foot and eventually managed to flag down a car, and the driver called the police and an ambulance. Do you remember that both Curtis Esmonde and Monica Stokes are dead?'

'So sad, such lovely people, they will be missed – not!' He was silent for a moment. Then he said, 'Shit, I'm sorry, darling. This is all my bloody fault.'

'Don't be silly! Your fault? No way.'

'How the hell did they find out where we were? That's what I'd like to know.' It was all coming back to him now. The photograph on the wall. 'They'd stayed at the hotel a couple of months ago. When did we decide to go there?'

'Back in February.'

'They must have found out, somehow.' He shrugged. 'We did all the bookings online – maybe they hacked us?'

'Maybe,' she agreed. 'I spoke to Glenn yesterday – he rang your phone – and I answered and told him what had happened. He made some calls, and said that neither Esmonde nor Stokes should ever have been released. All the time they were in prison they were telling other inmates they were going to get you when they came out. But do you want the good news?'

'There's good news?'

She grinned and nodded eagerly. 'Glenn went to see the Chief Constable. She's signed you off until you are fully recovered. So we can have a proper holiday now, and it's a really great place. I think you're going to love it. A beautiful old manor house – but really modern inside and lovely staff. There's an indoor and outdoor pool. Tennis courts. Bikes we can borrow. And it's surrounded by vineyards. Just gorgeous!'

'Sounds it.'

'And I have strict instructions from Glenn – you're not to even think about work. He's told me to take away your phone!'

'Cheeky bugger! Speaking of that, where is my phone? It needs charging.'

Cleo tapped her handbag. 'In here – and your thoughtful wife has charged it for you.'

He reached out with his right hand. 'Let me just have a quick look and check for anything urgent.'

She gave him a stern look.

'Just one quick check and then I'll switch the damned thing off,' Roy begged.

'Promise?'

'Scout's honour!'

With some reluctance, she dug in her bag and produced it. Just as she handed it to him, it pinged with the *new mail* tone. He stared at it for some moments, then grinned broadly. 'Well, look at this!'

'What is it?' she asked, suspiciously.

'It's an automated email from the chateau!'

'What?'

'From the wonderful Château-sur-L'Évêque! Asking if we've enjoyed our stay!'

'You are joking?'

Roy held the phone up and Cleo read the message aloud. '*The Vicomte and Vicomtesse du Carne de Chabrolais hope you have enjoyed your recent stay in our beautiful Château-sur-L'Évêque. We would be deeply obliged if you were to place your favourable comments in a review on TripAdvisor.*'

She handed the phone back to Roy and he read the message again himself. Then he gave her a playful look. 'Any thoughts?'

She rocked her head to one side, then the other. 'Um. Nothing's immediately jumping out at me. You?'

He nodded. 'Yes, I've got it. I know what to write.'

'Uh-huh?'

'*Visit the beautiful Château-sur-L'Évêque. Enjoy its isolation, its wonderful hospitality. Truly, you will have . . . the holiday to die for!*'

Acknowledgements

Writing any book involves a huge amount of teamwork, including those who help me with my research, with editing, the cover design, the marketing, the social media and so much more, and I've been blessed over the years to have the support of so many talented people.

First and foremost a huge thank you to Jojo Moyes, for her foresight and immense generosity in keeping the Quick Reads programme alive. These novellas play such a vital role in encouraging so many people who are either reading books for the first time or who have struggled or had lost the reading habit. And a huge thanks to Fanny Blake, my brilliant former editor at Penguin Signet – a few years back (!) – for twisting my arm to do this book, which has been a blast.

Those research helpers I would particularly like to single out on this novella are: Julian Blazeby, Connor Costen, Sean Didcott, Claire Horne, Manon Jones and Dr Adrian Noon.

Thank you also to my brilliant Team James readers, Sue Ansell, Martin Diplock, Jane Diplock, Anna-Lisa Hancock, James Hodge and Helen Shenston. To my agent, Isobel Dixon, Sian Ellis-Martin and all at Blake Friedmann, and to my publishers, Pan Macmillan, with a special mention to those who worked on this novella, Wayne Brookes, Samantha Fletcher, Alex Saunders, Lindsay Nash and Neil Lang. Huge thanks also to my publicists at Riot, Preena Gadher, Caitlin Allen and Emily Souders.

The inspiration for this story came from a hotel in central France that Lara and I stayed a night in a couple of years ago. The hotel was very much as I have described, incredibly creepy and old-fashioned, almost deserted and distinctly sinister – we really did think at one point we were going to end up murdered . . .

As ever, with this novella I've been helped enormously by my wife, Lara, both in recalling the details of the hotel and how we felt, and with all other aspects of the story. My good friend David Gaylor helped so much with both the front-line editing and the police aspects of the book, as well as cracking the whip to keep me to schedule!

Thanks also to our fabulous new PA, Kate

Blazeby; to our hardworking and always smiling finance manager, Sarah Middle; to Dani Brown, who does a terrific job running our social media; to Amy Robinson for her work with the team; and to her son Kit Robinson, the perfect model for Noah! And huge thanks to Chris Webb and Chris Diplock who keep our computers and all our tech going, and to Martin Walsh and Erin Brown who curate our video content.

And, as ever, a big thank you to our pets, who do so much to keep us sane: our dogs, Oscar, Spooky and Wally; our Burmese cats, Woo and Willy; our ducks, Mickey Magic, Clarissa, Locky, Maija, Bob, Barbara, Happy-Go-Ducky, Green Bean and a dozen more; our pygmy goats, Bouscaut, Margaux, Ted and Norman; our emus, Wolfie and Spike; and our alpacas, Alpacino, Fortescue, Jean-Luc, Boris and Keith. In a world that sometimes seems a little crazy and scary, none of these beautiful creatures has a care beyond ensuring they get their food and their treats: bones, carrots, blueberries, grapes, popcorn, ginger biscuits, sweetcorn and peas. Would that life should be so simple for us all!

My final word is to thank all of you, my readers. I always love to hear from you – your letters, emails, blog posts, tweets, Facebook, Instagram and YouTube comments are wonderful to receive.

contact@peterjames.com

www.peterjames.com

🐦 @peterjamesuk

f @peterjames.roygrace

You Tube peterjamesPJTV

📷 @peterjamesuk

📷 @peterjamesukpets

📷 @mickeymagicandfriends

QUICK READS

THE READING AGENCY

About Quick Reads

"Reading is such an important building block for success"
~ Jojo Moyes

Quick Reads are short books written
by best-selling authors.

Did you enjoy this Quick Read?

Tell us what you thought by
filling in our short survey.
Scan the **QR code** to go
directly to the survey or
visit **bit.ly/QR2023**

Thanks to Penguin Random House, Hachette and HarperCollins
and to all our publishing partners for their ongoing support.

A special thank you to Jojo Moyes for her generous donation
2020 - 2022 in support of Quick Reads.

Quick Reads is delivered by The Reading Agency, a national charity
tackling life's big challenges through the proven power of reading.

www.readingagency.org.uk   **@readingagency**   **#QuickReads**

The Reading Agency Ltd. Registered number: 3904882 (England & Wales)
Registered charity number: 1085443 (England & Wales)
Registered Office: 24 Bedford Row, London, WC1R 4EH
The Reading Agency is supported using public funding by
Arts Council England.

Supported using public funding by
ARTS COUNCIL ENGLAND

QUICK READS

Find your next Quick Read...

For 2023 we have selected 6 popular
Quick Reads for you to enjoy!

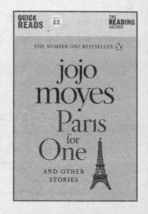

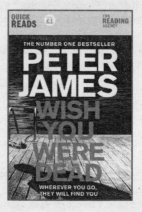

Quick Reads are available to buy in paperback or ebook
and to borrow from your local library. For a complete list
of titles and more information on the authors and their
books visit **www.readingagency.org.uk/quickreads**

THE READING AGENCY

Continue your reading journey with The Reading Agency

READING AHEAD

Challenge yourself to complete six reads by taking part in **Reading Ahead** at your local library, college or workplace: **readingahead.org.uk**

READING GROUPS FOR EVERYONE

Join **Reading Groups for Everyone** to find a reading group and discover new books: **readinggroups.org.uk**

Celebrate reading on **World Book Night** every year on 23 April: **worldbooknight.org**

SUMMER READING CHALLENGE

Read with your family as part of the **Summer Reading Challenge: summerreadingchallenge.org.uk**

For more information on our work and the power of reading please visit our website: **readingagency.org.uk**

More from Quick Reads

If you enjoyed the 2023 Quick Reads please explore our 8 titles from 2022.

For a complete list of titles and more information
on the authors and their books visit:
www.readingagency.org.uk/quickreads

Peter James's Detective Superintendent Roy Grace books in order:

Dead Simple
In the first Roy Grace novel, a harmless
stag-do prank leads to deadly consequences.

Looking Good Dead
It started with an act of kindness and
ended in murder.

Not Dead Enough
Can a killer be in two places at once?
Roy Grace must solve a case of stolen identity.

Dead Man's Footsteps
The discovery of skeletal remains in Brighton
sparks a global investigation.

Dead Tomorrow
In an evil world, everything's for sale.

Dead Like You
After thirteen years, has the notorious
'Shoe Man' killer returned?

Dead Man's Grip
A trail of death follows a devastating traffic accident.

Not Dead Yet
Terror on the silver screen; an obsessive
stalker on the loose.

Dead Man's Time
A priceless watch is stolen and the powerful Daly
family will do anything to get it back.

Want You Dead
Who knew online dating could be so deadly?

You Are Dead
Brighton falls victim to its first
serial killer in eighty years.

Love You Dead
A deadly black widow is on the hunt
for her next husband.

Need You Dead
Every killer makes a mistake somewhere.
You just have to find it.

Dead If You Don't
A kidnapping triggers a parent's worst nightmare
and a race against time for Roy Grace.

Dead At First Sight
Roy Grace exposes the lethal side
of online identity fraud.

Find Them Dead
A ruthless Brighton gangster is on trial
and will do anything to walk free.

Left You Dead
When a woman in Brighton vanishes without
a trace, Roy Grace is called in to investigate.

Picture You Dead
Not all windfalls are lucky. Some can lead to
murder . . .

Also by Peter James

Dead Letter Drop • Atom Bomb Angel

Billionaire • Possession • Dreamer

Sweet Heart • Twilight • Prophecy

Alchemist • Host • The Truth

Denial • Faith • Perfect People

The House on Cold Hill

Absolute Proof • The Secret of Cold Hill

I Follow You

Short Story Collection

A Twist of the Knife

Children's Novel

Getting Wired!

Novellas

The Perfect Murder

Wish You Were Dead

Non-Fiction

Death Comes Knocking: Policing Roy Grace's
Brighton (with Graham Bartlett)

Babes in the Wood (with Graham Bartlett)

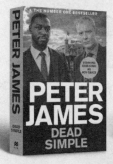
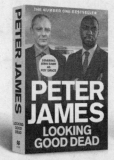
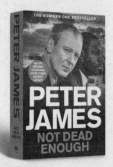
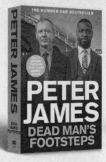
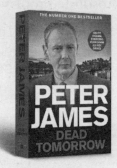